£1.25

MARCH HOUSE

The arrival of a mysterious new psychiatrist at March House, the psychiatric clinic where Ruth works, heralds the collapse of her entire world. Dr. Laver is flamboyant, vulgar, possibly even unethical—but he starts Ruth on an uneasy journey through the past, in which she glimpses her parents for the first time as separate people, in which her wholesome country life and the happy childhood she thought she had crumbles away to reveal something quite different.

Mary Hocking charts the transformation in the relationship between father and daughter, between Ruth and her colleagues, with great subtlety, drawing us further and further into this landscape of the mind till the final moving conclusion.

MARCH HOUSE

MARY HOCKING

1981

CHATTO & WINDUS

LONDON

Published by
Chatto & Windus Ltd
40 William IV Street
London WC2N 4DF

*

Clarke, Irwin & Co. Ltd
Toronto

British Library Cataloguing in Publication Data
    Hocking, Mary
      March House
      I. Title
      823'.914 [F]   PR6058.026

    ISBN 0-7011-2586-1

Printed in Great Britain by
Ebenezer Baylis & Son Ltd.
The Trinity Press, Worcester, and London

To BETH, DELIA,
MARGOT AND SUE

1

I DID not dress sombrely for my mother's funeral and one or two of my father's relatives were shocked. I heard them talking in the corridor while I was in the kitchen making tea.

'I'm surprised at Ruth; you would think she would have shown more respect for her father's sake.'

'They don't nowadays.'

'But she's always seemed an old-fashioned girl.'

My mother's sister, Eleanor, did not criticise. She was a short, prune-coloured woman with an air of watchful repose. Other people grew older, but she did not seem to have changed since I had first known her when she must have been in her twenties. Although she was plump, I was sure that for many years her weight had not varied by as much as a pound. There was nothing spontaneous about Eleanor; she thought carefully before she spoke and always gave the impression of holding something back. My father's eldest sister had told me yesterday that she feared Eleanor hoped to marry my father. I had no idea whether this was true or not; but, unlike my poor mother, Eleanor was a very intelligent woman, and whatever ambitions she might have had, she was keeping discreetly in the background today. I was aware, however, that she was watching me constantly, almost as though she found me as inexplicable as I found her. This surprised me as I have always thought of myself as a straightforward person.

Tomorrow the relatives were coming to lunch before returning to their respective parts of the country. I had prepared a cold buffet because I had to go back to work and would not be present. This shocked them even more than my not wearing sombre clothes.

My eldest aunt said, 'Your father needs you more than ever now.'

'He'll manage while you're all here,' I said cheerfully.

They did not like my being cheerful. But Mother had had a brain tumour and I had not felt that her death was a cause for sadness. I had been sad enough, though, before she died, but my father's relatives would not understand about that because none of them came to visit my mother when she was ill. They had never forgiven my father for marrying beneath him.

The house seemed heavy with death. The curtains had been drawn across the windows and although the wreaths which had been laid in the breakfast room had long since gone the scent of the flowers hung in the air. I could smell them all night, particularly the carnations. It was a relief to get out of the house the next morning.

My father was still asleep and I wheeled my bicycle across the front lawn so as not to make any noise which might disturb him. Before I rode away, I looked back at our home; an old red-brick house with a well-matured garden, fields in the distance and a few haphazard trees. My father chose to live in the country because he needed to escape from London and the responsibilities of his job at the Home Office. He did not want to gather up a lot of other responsibilities in the village, so he and my mother had lived a rather isolated life. Friends often asked whether I found it lonely, but I had always lived here and I had never thought about it. Today, however, I did find myself thinking it was odd that I lived in one isolated house and worked in another.

March House where we had our clinic was on the outskirts of the little town of Weston Market. It was a small country mansion which had been converted into a nursing home twenty years ago. When the nursing home failed, the Ainsworth Foundation took the building over. That was seven years ago, in the days when the Ainsworth Foundation was highly respected. The directors of the Foundation were Dr. Jonathan Ainsworth and his sister Olive. Dr. Ainsworth had made a simple discovery, namely that far more people are in need of psychiatric help than ever get to see a psychiatrist. In the commercial field this identification of a neglected human need might well have made a millionaire of a man as gifted and energetic as Dr. Ainsworth. As it was, thanks to his enterprise, clinics were set up in different parts of the country and for several years all went well. But unfortunately the number of people prepared to admit to this particular human need, let alone pay for its satisfaction, was in inverse ratio to the financial expectations of the professionals required to staff the clinics. Dr. Ainsworth, who was determined as well as being enterprising, gifted and energetic, engaged in a recruitment campaign of a somewhat eccentric nature which in due course attracted the attention of the British Medical Association and the police. The police had for the time being retired, but the British Medical Association was more tenacious and accusations relating to advertising were currently taking up a great deal of Dr. Ainsworth's time. Inevitably, the various establishments set up by Dr. Ainsworth suffered accordingly. When March House was first taken over by the Ainsworth Foundation there was a staff consisting of three psychiatric social workers, two clinical psychologists, two nurses, and a visiting psychiatrist who came three times a week. Now the professional staff was reduced to one clinical psychologist, one psychiatric social worker and a part-time nurse; the psychiatrist, whose visits had long been reduced to once a week, had retired and as yet no replacement had been appointed.

There were other problems, not of Dr. Ainsworth's

making. The clinic was supposed to have facilities for a limited number of residential patients and the psychiatric social worker, his wife and family, had lived on the premises thereby creating a warm, sheltered environment for the patients. The psychiatric social worker, however, had recently parted from his wife and family and formed a liaison with a male artist. As the directors of the Foundation had their own worries, it had not been thought necessary to burden them with this development; but it had been decided that the present relationship could not be regarded as a substitute for the nuclear family and so there was now no residential accommodation for patients.

When I entered the building the reception office, immediately to the right of the entrance hall, was empty and someone was buzzing impatiently for a line. I went into the room and studied the switchboard, which always looked very complicated to me although it was a comparatively simple model. The door of my room, on the left of the hall, was open and I could hear Iris Bailey, the clinical psychologist, talking to Mrs. Libnitz, the receptionist.

'Where *is* Ruth? She wasn't in yesterday and . . .'

'It was her mother's funeral.' Mrs. Libnitz, a wiry little Jugoslav, always tended to sound angry; now she made it apparent that she was shocked as well.

Iris took up the challenge immediately. 'The death of a husband, a child, *that* is a tragedy; but the death of a mother is something that comes to us all.'

'The death of a mother strikes to the heart.' Mrs. Libnitz spoke with a venom that robbed the statement of all pathos.

These two hated each other. Mrs. Libnitz was a refugee and needed someone to hate; but I could never understand why Iris should reciprocate. Now she said in an amused voice calculated to annoy, 'Well, I hope Ruth

10

isn't too stricken. Did we send flowers?'

'We sent a donation to the Brain Research Fund or some such place.'

'Oh yes, I remember.'

'And Douglas went to the funeral.' Mrs. Libnitz laid accusing emphasis on 'Douglas'.

'*Did* he? I don't think he mentioned it to me. But as long as we were represented . . . Will Ruth be back today? Not that we want to hurry her; but I expect she'd like to have something to occupy her mind. And in any case, I *must* have Mrs. Walsh's file, the court hearing is tomorrow.'

'I am back, Iris,' I called out.

Iris came into the room, arms outstretched. She laid her hands on my shoulders and studied me gravely. Behind her I could see Mrs. Libnitz making a sour face.

'You're all right?' Iris nodded her head, having satisfied herself without the need for a reply. 'Of course you are. That's my girl!'

Mrs. Libnitz elbowed past us and flipped up the switch on the board, cutting off the speaker. As Iris and I went out of the room we could hear her having an altercation about private calls with Di Brady, the nurse. We went across the corridor to my room. Iris said, 'That woman always makes me feel as though I have just made the most inexcusable mistake, possibly costing several lives.'

'I expect every office has these problems.'

She looked at me. Her eyes were large and colourless, expressive windows for whatever aspect of her personality she wished to put on display. 'But this *isn't* every office. We ought to be able to manage our personal relationships better than that.' I thought as I looked at her that there was something formidable about the impact of foaming white hair on a face suntanned and still young, a face bright with certainty, knowing nothing of the chastening of age. Iris was attractive now in her early

11

forties, but already little lines at the sides of the incisive mouth and incipient pouches beneath the square jaw gave warning that in later life pugnacity might make her appearance less agreeable.

I said, 'Perhaps we make too much of things which would pass unnoticed elsewhere?' It was no use discussing, let alone arguing, with Iris, yet I always persisted.

'But the more one notices, the more one understands, surely? Or are you saying that our relationships are fragile?'

I took the cover off my typewriter and a pile of papers which had been placed underneath slid onto the floor.

'Sensitive, certainly,' Iris said, 'but not fragile.' She gave a satisfied nod. While I tidied up the papers she went over to the filing cabinet. There was something impatient about the way she walked, head slightly bowed, arms moving as though she was elbowing her way through a crowded market. I had noticed when I saw her out walking with her sons that she always kept a pace ahead of them as though competing in a race. She was a very competitive person. Today, the competitiveness irritated me and I wanted to say, 'What's it all about, Iris? If you'd only stand still you'd realise how far ahead of the field you are.'

She was under five foot, but generously endowed with full, deep breasts and ample thighs, a cottage loaf figure. She was almost ludicrously sexy and could have been as formidable as she wished with very little cost to herself if she had just been content with the way Nature had made her. Instead, she scorned her sex and was obsessed with a power struggle at the clinic; but the pathetic thing was that no one was opposing her only she did not seem to realise this.

'You *are* all right?' She had turned from the filing cabinet and was looking at me; I had been away for several days and I could see that she was counting the cost of my absence, and possible future absences if things were not all right. 'How is your father? Did he cope? I'm sure *you* coped, you always do.'

I looked at the pile of work on my desk, trying to ignore a tightening of my stomach muscles; I was suddenly unsure whether I had coped and would cope in the future. Iris glanced at the papers in her hand; she was obviously reluctant to ask about them so soon after mentioning my bereaved father and looked like a child who is being disciplined.

'Is it Mrs. Walsh's file that you want?' I asked, taking pity on her. 'It is in Douglas's room. Jimmy Powell from probation came to see him the other day about Len Walsh.'

'Really, that's too bad of Douglas. I told him I couldn't find the file anywhere only yesterday.'

'Douglas has a lot on his mind,' I pointed out.

Iris seemed reluctant to concede that any part of the answer to Douglas's behaviour might lie outside his work; she allowed her work to absorb her whole life and imagined that other people were the same. 'It's not having a psychiatrist,' she said. 'He's been going downhill ever since Dr. Arnold left. But things are getting crucial now. He has begun to withdraw from me. Yesterday, when I went in to talk to him about the Walsh case he sat at his desk looking at me as though inwardly he was cowering in the corner of the room.'

'Perhaps he had had a row with Eddie?' I suggested.

'It's a trying time, I know. Not having a psychiatrist is worrying for all of us.'

'I think *you* manage very well.' She gave the impression of enjoying getting on with her cases without the intervention of a psychiatrist.

'But Douglas always folds up under pressure. He needs support.'

13

'Dr. Arnold wasn't much of a support.'

'But when he was around Douglas knew where his own responsibility stopped. Now it's too much for him.'

'I would have thought Douglas had shown himself fairly resilient to responsibility.'

'We mustn't make judgements, Ruth.'

'It was just an observation.' I threaded paper into my typewriter. 'Do you want these case reports done first, or the appointment letters?'

'The appointment letters.'

I put the appointment letters on top of the pile and asked casually, 'Did you write to the Foundation while I was away?'

'No. I think we need to have something constructive to suggest before we write.' Douglas, on announcing his altered circumstances, had proposed that he should move out of the clinic and that Iris and her family should move in — to preserve the 'homely atmosphere'. From the little which Iris had subsequently said, it seemed that her family felt that enough sacrifices had already been demanded of them on the altar of psychiatry and were not prepared for further involvement.

'After all,' Iris said, 'we don't know how long this silliness of Douglas's will last.'

'Have you met Eddie?' I asked.

'I sometimes doubt if he exists!'

When Douglas's friend moved in, one damp February evening, Douglas told us that he was looking forward to meeting us very much; but after several weeks, during which, if one walked quietly into the residential wing of the building, one might see a shadow flit out of view, or hear a door shut fast, it became apparent that the friend was taking good care not to meet us.

'He exists all right,' I said. 'He smokes those foul French cigarettes.'

'I find the whole thing a trifle sinister,' Iris said.

14

'It is not sinister at all.' Mrs. Libnitz had come in, un-observed, with the post. 'He wants Douglas to himself so he pretends that none of you exist.'

Iris looked at Mrs. Libnitz, eyebrows raised. 'You've been boning up on your psychology, Mrs. Libnitz,' she said, adopting her amusedly tolerant voice.

'I don't know anything about psychology,' Mrs. Libnitz retorted. 'I just know people.' She went out, also knowing a good exit line.

'You must have a talk with Douglas, Ruth,' Iris said. 'You're always so splendid with him; the last time he was bad you were the one person who could do anything with him.'

'Only because I didn't try to do anything with him, Iris.'

'Well, try now; before he really puts up the shutters.'

The telephone rang and I picked up the receiver, but it was someone who wanted the dairy. Our telephones were frequently out of order and we got a lot of crossed lines; lately, we had had people telephoning who were waiting for taxis. Communication was not good. Postal deliveries had been erratic and one bag of mail had been found recently in the village pond. This made us all a bit edgy, particularly Iris who was convinced that the letter saying the new psychiatrist was on his way was now lying at the bottom of the pond. While I was speaking on the telephone Iris examined the post speculatively. There was one white envelope and two brown ones. When I put down the receiver she said to me, 'The white envelope, I should think. Open the brown ones first; we'll save our treat to the last.'

The first brown envelope contained a misdirected salary slip; the second a letter from Norfolk Social Services Department demanding a reply to a letter. 'We haven't had any reports from them on Victor Mullani,' Iris said. 'In fact, I'm sure we haven't got a Victor

Mullani among our treasures.' She put the letter aside and watched while I opened the white envelope. There was a letter inside from the London headquarters of the Foundation; it stated briefly that Dr. Laver, consultant psychiatrist, would be starting with us in ten days' time. There was no date on the letter. I looked at the postmark on the envelope but it was illegible. Iris was very excited and hurried out of the office to tell Di.

When I had finished the case reports that I was typing I telephoned the County clinic which had a helpful secretary and asked her if she knew anything about Dr. Laver.

'Dr. Laver?' It was a bad line and I could not hear her very well. 'You're sure it says Dr. Laver?'

I said I was sure. She said, 'What about Dr. Laver?' It was a bad line, she said, she could hardly hear me. We did not talk for long.

I typed uninterrupted for an hour and then Di Brady came to have coffee with me. She walked to the window seat, moving with the relaxed, slouching gait which had so distracted Dr. Arnold, and sat down, stretching long legs in front of her. Her uniform was a tight fit and the skirt rode up when she sat down. 'How are things with you?' she asked. 'Iris says we have a new psychiatrist. He'd better be good. I'm fed up.'

'No work?'

She nodded, staring with heavy-lidded eyes into her cup. The lack of residential patients had meant that there was much less for her to do and she was bored. Also, she felt 'it isn't moral, what's happening here.'

'I'd feel I ought to say something only I've got the kids to support and this is a job near home.' She nibbled a bun, brooding on this. 'If I made a fuss they'd have me out of here damn quick. Let's face it, I only got the job because no one else applied.'

'What made you take up nursing, Di?'

'All those doctors on telly. Look where it got me.'

'Isn't Alec with you?'

'He left me again last night.' Tears came into her eyes; she was easily hurt and prone to put herself in a position where she was likely to be hurt. 'Why do things go sour so soon?' She shifted her position on the window seat slightly. Her short, corn-coloured hair was rumpled as though she had just tumbled out of bed and the flat, generous planes of her face were untouched by make-up, although I could smell body oil. 'You find a fellow who's grateful to you just for breathing and suddenly it's all over and he treats you like shit.'

'You'll find another bloke, Di.'

'It's not easy, with two kids.'

The door opened and Douglas Gulliver came in. It was his practice to have coffee in my room, sitting on the window seat, and he looked disconcerted to find Di there. She gazed at him from beneath drooping eyelids. I examined him more directly. He had a cap of sleek black hair and a round, pale face like a rather sad pudding; horn-rimmed spectacles protected puzzled brown eyes. I had always felt sorry for Douglas because I had imagined that he was too gentle to look after his own interests. This was how he affected most women, Di included. Now that he had left his wife I was revising my opinion of him; I wasn't sure how Di felt.

'Sometimes I get very tired of rural life,' he said disconsolately stirring his coffee. 'I went into the village shop for cigarettes and half the cast of the Archers was there, chewing the cud in their bovine way. You know what was exercising their minds? They were listening to old Appleton reciting a long list of items he *didn't* stock and how much each would cost if he had stocked it. Every so often he had to look up a catalogue to refresh his memory, and they all stood ruminating on this great issue while I was waiting for my cigarettes.'

Di said, 'I've got a packet you can have.' Involvement was important to her, she saw no other point in conversation. 'When did you take up smoking?'

'I haven't. I said I'd get some for Eddie.' He frowned as though the light hurt his eyes. 'Sometimes I wonder if this place isn't just a mistake; one of those places which exists without anyone knowing anything about it because someone made a mistake on a map. County A thinks the boundary stops to the south while County B thinks it stops to the north; we are in a narrow strip which has been forgotten for centuries. It probably goes back to the time of the ancient kingdoms. After all, this *is* March House; and doesn't March mean "a boundary or debatable strip between countries"?' He was only half-joking; he never seemed very sure of the ability of the world to reassemble itself each day.

Di said, 'Christ! It's not the clients who need the new psychiatrist!'

'New psychiatrist?' He looked at her directly for the first time. She smiled, glad to give pleasure, and told him that Iris had said we had a new psychiatrist as though this was her own personal gift to him.

'When is he starting?' Douglas seemed, if anything, rather taken aback. Perhaps he had hoped for more time to sort out his affairs.

'We're not quite sure,' I said. 'There's no date on the letter.' I handed the letter to Douglas and Di came across to read it, leaning against his shoulder. 'You happy now?' she asked.

He moved away irritably and put the letter back on my desk. 'I suppose it will look neater if we have the full complement. Apart from that we don't seem to have any more success when we have a psychiatrist.'

He went out of the room and Di stared after him. 'If it wasn't for the kids I wouldn't stay in the place,' she said. 'But Iris runs it better than any health administrator I ever came across, and Douglas isn't a bad social worker. So who gets harmed? That's what I say to myself.'

'What does Mrs. Libnitz make of it?' I wondered.

'She wouldn't realise things were different anywhere else, would she?'

So that left me. I went along with it because they had been good with time off when Mother was ill.

Iris came in after lunch and said that we must start making preparations for the new psychiatrist. We were short of current clients and she did not want him to be discouraged. 'Perhaps you could go through the register and make a list of the clients we have lost touch with. Then Douglas and I can do a bit of visiting.'

Mrs. Libnitz came in while I was working on the list and said the new psychiatrist would have enough to do here without any clients.

I had a busy day and it was twenty past six when I left the office. I should have been prepared for what happened then, but I wasn't. For over a year the office had been a place where I was released from myself. So serious to Iris, to me the events there had the quality of a charade which I observed and which helped me to forget reality. But now, reality had changed; it was still at home, waiting for me, but it was different. I felt frightened as I pedalled down the lane. I had felt anxious while my mother was ill, wondering what had happened during the day, but not frightened. Why should I be frightened now? It was over, wasn't it?

My father was already at home when I arrived, he had caught an early train. Usually he was not home until quite late; he had always said the only time he could get any useful work done was after four in the afternoon. He seemed to have expected me to leave early as well this afternoon. 'You're not usually so late, surely?' he asked. We had never talked much about my work and now he said, 'You don't do evening surgery?'

'I don't work for the doctors any more,' I laughed. 'I've been working at the clinic for three years now.'

He stared at me anxiously as though my behaviour perplexed him. 'I was worried,' he said.

'Worried?' I felt he expected some kind of apology from me and this irritated me. 'But I'm often home later than this if I go into town on my way.'

I hung up my coat and went into the kitchen to make preparations for our meal. He followed and stood in the doorway, watching me.

'I was thinking about a holiday,' he said. 'Things have been so hard for you. Would you like to go to Scotland? You have always said you wanted to explore Ross and Cromarty. We might take a cottage up there.'

'I only have three weeks' leave,' I pointed out.

'We could go for a fortnight. That would leave you a week for anything else you wanted to do.'

My holidays were usually spent keeping up with my friends who had scattered fairly widely; three weeks had never seemed long enough.

My father said, 'Of course, I know you like to see Dorothy.'

He did not say any more. These withdrawals into silence had always had a disastrous effect on my mother who either capitulated or let out a torrent of angry abuse: my father knew that I was not given to angry outbursts. I broke eggs into a bowl and whisked vigorously. In the past I had been an intermediary between my mother and my father and I was unused to this more direct relationship. If anyone had asked me a year ago whether I would have managed better living alone with my father or with my mother, I would have said with my father. Now I felt rather at a loss with him. But this, after all, was bound to be a difficult time. He had come home from work for the first time since Mother died and I could understand the enormous emptiness with only me there in the kitchen. I felt it myself, as though a great crowd of people had melted away and left my father and me alone, unprepared for and even a little shocked by our isolation. During my mother's illness we had grieved in different ways and had not been able to comfort each other. Now we were neither of us quite sure how the other felt. It was harder for my father; he had to construct another life and no doubt needed rather urgently to find out how I was going to fit into it. I wasn't sure myself, so I hoped that tonight I could concentrate on practical things like preparing food, eating and washing up.

To my relief, my father said, 'Oh well, I'll leave you to think about it.' He was looking at the clock which told him that any further conversation would delay dinner until half-past eight by which time he hoped to be watching a programme on an archaeological site in Turkey.

Our springer spaniel, Punter, barked at the back door and I let him in. He seemed anxious, too, and followed me about the kitchen as though he was afraid to let me out of his sight.

Over supper, my father raised the question of a holiday again. 'I can understand that you must want to see Dorothy and your other friends.'

'Well, yes . . .'

'Why don't you take some time off now and go to Dorothy? Things have been difficult these last few months and you need a break. I can manage for a week or so.'

'I can't take weeks off just like that.' I was surprised; as a civil servant he must have known the position regarding compassionate leave as well as I did. 'Besides, Dorothy teaches.'

'What has that to do with it?'

'There wouldn't be any point in going to her during term-time.'

'Really?' The perplexed look came into his face again. He had such a quick mind that it was disconcerting to see him so unable to grasp simple facts. We ate in silence. I felt tired and flat and could not think of anything to say. Later, I would have to clear some of the things from my mother's room and the thought oppressed me.

When we were having coffee, my father said, 'I know that when your mother was alive it was important for you to get out of the house and occupy yourself with other people; but now that things are different, is it necessary for you to go out to work?'

'But I must work.'

'Why? You refused to go to university.' It was extraordinary how quickly he picked me up on this, as though the refusal had been made only yesterday and the resentment was still warm. 'I remember that on the advice of the school we sent you to an educational psychologist and he said you weren't motivated, or some such nonsense.'

'But that was different.'

'You are motivated now?'

It had not been possible to explain my attitude at the time and I could hardly expect to succeed now, but I said, 'I didn't want a profession. But I must have a job. I'm over thirty.'

'I fail to see what your age has to do with it.'

'I'm a grown woman; I have to have a job.'

'I should have thought,' he said, after a pause during which he made a wry grimace as though this was rather beyond him, 'that a woman *doesn't* have to have a job, unlike a man.'

I realised he was making arrangements for me to take over my mother's role and I was annoyed that he should do it so clumsily. But then I thought that it showed how unsettled he must be by my mother's death, even a little frightened. I had never thought of my father, who was always quiet and unemotional, as a frightened person. I suppose we didn't know each other very well. His face was composed now, but the eyes had a startled, affronted look I had not seen before. I felt dismayed and was about to offer to go to Scotland with him when the telephone rang.

He went to answer it and stayed in the hall for several minutes. When he came back, he said, 'That was Eleanor.' He gave me a reproachful look as though I had let him down over some matter in which Eleanor was involved.

2

THERE was a beautiful view from the back of our house across fields and orchards with no buildings in sight. My bedroom and the spare bedroom, in which my father had slept for the last year, were at the back of the house. Mother had insisted on a bedroom at the front of the house because she liked to look down the lane towards the farm cottages and outbuildings. These buildings were not old or picturesque, but Mother had liked buildings whatever their architectural merit; when there was a scheme for a housing development in the vicinity she had refused to sign a petition which opposed it on the grounds that it would spoil the rural nature of the area. 'Shit the rural nature of the area!' she had said to my father, though to the woman presenting the petition she had said she had mislaid her glasses; she did not wear glasses.

'You should have the courage of your convictions,' my father had said in his gently mocking way.

'I don't have convictions. I have feelings. But no one in this place cares about feelings.'

I pushed open the door of her room.

The big sash window had been open at the bottom all day, but the room still smelt sour. I stripped the bed and put the sheets and blankets in the linen basket on the landing. Then I took the mattress off the bed and propped it against a chair under the windows. In the morning I would ask Mrs. James, our daily woman, to help me carry it down to the garden; the weather was fine and I could leave it out on the lawn all day. The rug and the carpet were stained. I wanted to roll them up and get them out into the fresh air, too, but I managed to restrain myself. There would be time to do these things, there wasn't any need to tear the room apart.

The pictures, picked up from stalls in Camden Passage before it became fashionable, were dusty, the glass spotted. The mirror with a picture of Carole Lombard painted on it was spotted, too, and the silver on the dressing-table was tarnished; the lacquered top was smeared. A bottle of scent was lying on its side, leaking Ma Griffe through the stopper. The last few months of her illness had been very difficult and my father, Eleanor and I had exhausted ourselves trying to make her comfortable day and night. But now that all the activity was over, the uncared-for objects in the room seemed like a reproach and I began to accuse myself. I had imagined the aftermath of death as an exhausted, but ultimately healing, sorrow, but in fact it was more unpleasant than that: mingled with guilt was anger, though what I was angry about I would have found it hard to say.

There was a pile of letters and cards on the bedside-table with messages which varied from 'Get better soon, Lil' to 'I am with you always, even to the end of time'. I tidied them and put them on the landing-table so that I would not forget to take them down to the drawing-room; there were people to whom I must write expressing thanks for their kind thoughts. I examined the various tablets which had done so little to relieve her distress and decided to cope with them later.

While I did these things I was not thinking much about Mother; I just wanted to make the room less dreadful because I could not sleep another night while it was in this state. I began to take her clothes out of the wardrobe and while I did this I caught myself thinking that there would be more room for my own things when I had got them out of the way. The thought horrified me; it was not even as though I had anything much to store, clothes did not interest me. My father was downstairs watching television. He had not asked me how I was going to spend the evening, although I think he guessed. He had said earlier that he could not bear to touch her things, an attitude which seemed more appropriate than mine. I seemed to have lost not only my mother but the feeling part of myself.

Punter came and stood in the doorway. I think he would have been happier if my father and I had stayed in the same room so that he could have kept an eye on both of us. I reassured him and he went downstairs and barked outside the sitting-room door. Father said, 'If you come in, you're not going out again.'

· I finished taking the clothes out of the wardrobe. They presented a problem. Most of them were unsuitable for country wear. I realised, as I looked at them hung about the room, how little Mother had adapted to the changes in her life.

My mother was born Lillian Jacobs and she lived all her life until she married in the flat above her father's clothes' shop in Islington. Eleanor had told me that when Mother was young she was so lovely she stopped the traffic. Even in later years, when she had put on weight and had to dye her hair to keep it blonde, she was an arresting person. In contrast, my father seemed always to be trying to merge into the background; he was tall and thin and good-looking in a fastidious, apologetic way, and he looked faintly tired about the eyes. Mother seemed to have been over-endowed with physical energy and vitality but had not been given a corresponding sense of purpose. Father had an air of quiet certainty, but life seemed a puzzle to Mother. She got very angry and could never make people understand why, and she tended to leave sentences unfinished as though afraid to see her thoughts through to a conclusion. She was very demonstrative and loving but never received enough in return to satisfy her and so she was often hurt. She had no friends in the village. My father thought this was perverse of her.

'You are always complaining of being lonely, but you won't attend any of the village functions.'

'If I went I'd still be lonely. I'd be on my own.'

'Take Ruth with you.'

'Ruth isn't a man. I couldn't go without a man, I'd feel humiliated.'

'Well, my dear, if you won't go to these village functions on your own there's nothing we can do about it. When I get home from the office I want to get away from people, not go out and rub shoulders with them. I'm not gregarious. You are the one who likes company. Why don't you have a tea party?'

'Tea party! I wouldn't know what to say to *them*.'

The country folk depressed her and, in some way that I could not understand, she found them threatening. She was not a cultured woman, so she could not mix with the wealthy families in the neighbourhood, most of whom were not cultured either but would have died rather than admit it.

Poor Mother! I looked at the black cocktail dress with the satin tie. Her clothes had always seemed to make statements for her. This dress, worn in the garden, had said, 'Look how bored I am in your wretched garden!' The garden was his particular joy; he worked hard in it and longed for her appreciation. 'It was such a lovely afternoon,' he would say. 'Did you sit out in the garden?' She would stare dully at him as though he was talking in a foreign language. On the rare occasions when she joined him in the garden for any length of time she would always wear something that made her look out of place.

'All you care about is London,' I often heard him say.

'The people in London are alive.'

Certainly, she was alive in London. To my father's embarrassment, she had conversations with people on buses, in the street, in shops. She would see someone who looked lost and hurry forward to give advice and directions, she would ask newspaper vendors what sort of a day they had had, she could not move away from a kiosk without an exchange of views on the changing nature of the town, she spent precious minutes talking to the coloured women attendants in public lavatories while my father waited miserably outside. In the end, he refused to meet her in London. 'I have enough of it all day.' So once a week she went up to London on her own. I remember asking her once what she had done that day.

'I walked.'

'But where?'

'Just anywhere.' She looked at me, clenching her hands, on the verge of the unreasonable anger which so often flared up. 'God! You don't understand, do you, my own child and you don't even begin to understand! In London I can walk along the street, any street, and no one knows me; I don't have to explain myself to anyone . . .'

'But you don't have to explain yourself here.'

'All the bloody time!'

'It's because you're a Londoner you feel so at home there,' I temporised.

' "You feel you're at home there",' she mimicked. Although she was not clever, she was very quick to catch a meaning even before the speaker was fully aware of it. She began to sing an exaggerated, sentimental parody of 'London Pride'. I laughed because she did this kind of thing well, and she laughed, too, her anger forgotten. She took my hand and squeezed it. 'Oh, duckie, let me try . . . There was this little street off Camden High Street . . . I hadn't noticed it before, though goodness knows I've walked down that high street often enough . . . but there it was, half-a-dozen terraced houses, so quiet you could tuck yourself away there and no one would know . . . And yet a few hundred yards away there was the High Street and all the lovely Cypriot shops, the greengrocers and the delicatessens; and all the people coming and going; people you'd pass once and never see again. I could just imagine myself in one of those little houses, with a bed close by the window, lying there, listening to it, all that bustle and hustle, not needing to go out if I didn't want to, just having it all come in through the window. . . .' She closed her eyes and tears trickled down her cheeks. 'Perhaps in the evening the smell from the restaurant would tempt me . . .' Her plump fist clenched against her breast. She looked so bereft that I wanted to comfort her, but had no idea what it was that she needed.

'Did you get your dress?' I asked.

She pushed my hand away, recognising that I was treating her like a child and asking her to show me her pretty things. 'No, I didn't get a dress. I just walked. You've got a silly mother, Ruth.'

Sometimes when she set out on a weekly visit she would say she was going to the theatre, but she never went. Occasionally, she met one of her family, but most often she walked, or sat alone in a café taking a long time over a meal.

'Oh Mother, why?' Suddenly I was crying quietly. 'Why? Why . . . ?' I could no more have finished that sentence than she could have done.

The tears gave me a headache but brought no relief. I wasn't even sure what it was that needed relief. My eyes and throat ached and when I went to bed I could not sleep. The air was oppressive, and some time after midnight the curtains stirred and a flash of lightning lit up the room. The thunder was still distant. The door of my father's room opened and I heard him walk along the landing to the bathroom. I wondered whether he had a headache, too. Heavy drops of rain plopped on the window sill, on the leaves of the trees. Downstairs, Punter began to whine. My father went downstairs and soon I heard them both coming upstairs. My father said softly outside my door, 'Are you awake, Ruth?'

I said, 'M'yes,' making my voice sound sleepy.

'There's a storm coming up. Better close your window.'

I said that I would, but I left the window open and lay listening to the rain which was now falling steadily. The curtains billowed out like a wind-sock. The smell of wet earth was pleasant but the air was still heavy.

The storm circled around but did not come directly overhead. The wind rattled doors and wood creaked. Amidst all this noise I sometimes imagined that I heard the floorboards creaking in my father's room and I wondered if he was upset and whether I should go to him. I remained propped up in bed, watching the lightning flashes briefly lighting up the garden and wondering why I did not go to him.

3

A C R O S S the fields from the clinic, its chimneys visible between trees, stood the Mill House which had been in the ownership of the same family for over two hundred years. The present occupant was the last of the line and played the part with sufficient force to ensure that the name would survive long after her death. As a child I could remember seeing Miss Maud Leveridge dressed even then a little eccentrically, but still acceptably because at that time she was elegant and only part dotty and could carry off what were regarded as 'arty' clothes. Now, probably in her seventies and considerably more eccentric, Miss Maud wore the same long flowered gowns, much faded, torn and mud-stained. Her hair was dyed a rusty black and her thin, fine features were made up in the exaggerated style of the thirties' movies. She lived alone except for her cats whose company she pre-ferred to that of human beings. The clinic staff were her nearest neighbours and she paid us constant visits. She told us that over the years she had murdered more men than she could remember in the Mill House. When she was not telling us about the men she had murdered, she was giving advice to our clients. She was doing this when I arrived on Thursday morning, having first delivered a report to one of the local doctors. It was half-past nine. One of Iris's clients was sitting outside the reception room with her teenage daughter.

Miss Maud, wearing a mangled straw hat and a long, ominous purple dress, was advising the client, 'My dear, he's writing out a prescription before you walk in the room, now isn't he?'

31

Mrs. Libnitz, who did not believe that her job involved her in any loyalty to the health service, nodded in vigorous agreement.

'Drugs,' Miss Maud went on, 'are as much a mystery to the G.P. as the source of his spells are to the witch doctor. As far as he is concerned, they have one magic power: they enable him to do his surgery without actually examining any of his patients. Did Dr. Jones examine you?'

'No, but . . .'

'Then tear up that prescription.' She tweaked a piece of paper from the teenager's hand and tore it in pieces.

'That was my raffle ticket!'

'All you need is out there.' Miss Maud pointed out of the window. 'Nature provides the cure: the drug companies make it expensive, that's the only difference.'

'Now you're being very naughty, Miss Maud.' Iris hurried out of her room to claim her client. 'What's this that you've torn up?'

'It's my raffle ticket!'

'Raffle ticket? You shouldn't be spending your pennies on raffle tickets, Sharon.'

'I sold it to her.' Mrs. Libnitz pushed her head through the enquiry hatch.

'You shouldn't be selling tickets on these premises . . .'

'It's for multiple sclerosis . . .'

'I don't mind what it's for . . .'

Miss Maud watched this little scene which she had set up with satisfaction. I walked quietly across to my room, but it was no use; she pounced on me before I could close the door.

'When is the new psychiatrist starting?'

'New psychiatrist?'

'Yes, yes, of course I know you have a new psychiatrist.' She followed me into the room. 'Why are you so secretive about it? His name ought to be proclaimed in the stars, or at least put up on the notice board.'

'Miss Maud, you know you don't trust doctors . . .'

'But I love psychiatrists. They are so amusing. When can I meet this one?'

'You want an appointment?'

'Now don't be clever with me, child, because I'm much more clever than you are. I just want to come and have a chat with him. After all, we are both in the same line of business. I, too, am a healer.'

I wanted to say, 'what about all those men you murdered?' but I was a little afraid to take on Miss Maud; it was quite true that she was more clever than I was. I think she was more clever than Dr. Arnold.

'I don't know when he is starting,' I said. 'You'll probably know before we do, Miss Maud.'

'It would be nice if he would call on me. But the days of old-fashioned courtesy have gone. Nevertheless, perhaps you will tell him that I shall be glad if he will join me in a glass of wine, say, next Wednesday, at twelve o'clock?'

'I'll make a note of it.'

She watched me write it down. Then she said, 'Now that your mother is dead, do you intend to go on working in this place?'

I looked at her, too startled to speak.

'It's a frightful waste. You do realise that, don't you? Simply frightful.'

'Waste?'

'Of *you*, child. Get right away from here.'

'I can't leave my father,' I said involuntarily, not meaning to enter into a discussion with her.

'Hate your father!' she said vehemently. 'It's too late to hate your mother; but hate your father. Don't you know your commandments? He talked a lot of sense, you know; as well as saying some rather silly things.'

She turned away abruptly and left the room. In the corridor I could hear Mrs. Libnitz saying to Douglas, 'I'd like to see it in writing . . .'

'I shouldn't let it trouble you, Mrs. Libnitz.'

'I'm not troubled. But she said I shouldn't sell them on the premises and I'd like to see it in writing . . .'

'Perhaps it would be better not to sell them to the clients?'

'Does it say so in writing?'

'I've no idea.' Douglas came into my room and shut the door.

'You've just missed Miss Maud,' I told him.

He sat down in the armchair which was usually reserved for clients who were waiting.

'You're going to visit Mrs. Harrison at ten,' I reminded him.

'What am I doing advising Mrs. Harrison? Her husband has left home because he couldn't put up with Mrs. Harrison and the four children any longer. What am I supposed to say? That I know exactly how he feels?'

'Poor Mrs. Harrison. She didn't produce four children unaided, did she?'

'She likes babies. As soon as the youngest gets past the baby stage, she wants another. Charlotte was just the same.'

'Maybe Mrs. Harrison feels she is good with babies?'

'Why don't you see her for me? You would do it much better. You have so much sympathy for her.'

I did not answer. He watched me, biting his lip. He was in one of those moods when he seemed to warn others to keep their distance and yet looked at them with eyes which begged something of them. Women found him hard to resist and I was no exception. He said quietly, 'You do sympathise with Charlotte, don't you?'

'Yes, I do.'

'It hasn't been easy for me, Ruth.'

'I can't help feeling sorry for her and the children.'

'There are things you don't know.'

I was silent and he said, 'You are very obstinate in your quiet way; I would hate to have a battle of wills with you.' He was angry that his appeal had failed. His expressive eyes had gone very dark and I was afraid of what he might say. He could be spiteful when he was hurt. He said, 'I suppose you haven't had enough experience to realise that life isn't all black and white. If there is one thing marriage does for a person, it makes them tolerant of failure.'

'Mea culpa, Douglas. I didn't mean to be un-sympathetic.'

'Which is just another way of saying that you don't sympathise, of course. It's hard for you to understand about me and Charlotte. Your parents were very devoted, no doubt.'

I began to type a court report. He sat in the chair, watching me. 'What goes on in your head, I wonder?' he mused. 'You do the work impeccably and you bear with our faults; you are sympathetic to the clients but never intrusive; you are, as your reference said, a model of "patience, good humour and discretion". You demand very little for yourself, except privacy.'

'Is that bad? Privacy?'

'You are a very private person, and this makes me wonder whether you aren't also rather self-concerned.'

I finished the page and replaced the carbons. Douglas got up and went out of the room. My concentration wavered. Douglas and I had developed an odd, uneasy relationship and for some reason that I could not under-stand he seemed to observe me in order to find a weak-ness in my capacity for giving and then expose it. He had told me that as well as being intolerant I was self-concerned. What bloody cheek! I thought, mangling the paper as I wound it into the machine. Self was what this clinic was all about: self-knowledge allowing self-forgiveness from which would come self-awareness leading to self-reliance culminating in self-fulfilment. What was wrong with a little self-concern? Our clients were all people who were having trouble with self; women with children preventing their self-fulfilment and husbands with demands in conflict with the woman's own needs; the husbands themselves prevented from developing self to the full by their marital ties, the financial burden of home, wife, children. Even the people who were free of all that and lived together without admitting any ties or responsibility had trouble fulfilling themselves. In a world full of people constantly impinging on one another it is very difficult to help people to preserve their selfhood intact. If I had gone some way to preserving mine, Douglas should surely have applauded me.

While I worked this over in my mind, I knew that I should not have been upset by Douglas's reproach if it had not brought to mind my resistance to my father's wish that we should go on holiday together.

I had refused to go to university. There had been such tension about that, I had forgotten how bad it had been until my father brought it up again. But why should I be so distressed about it now? I hadn't liked Douglas giving me a run-down on my character. At the clinic I was an observer; an observer isn't part of the charade; I didn't want them to try to draw me into it, make me participate. I wasn't going to have that any more than I was going to university. There was a connection missing somewhere in my thought process, but that was something that had never bothered me in the past; the difference was that this time instead of confusing other people I was confusing myself.

Iris poked her head round the door to say that she was taking Mrs. Haines to the hospital for an appointment.

'Do you want to sign this report before you go?'

She came into the room followed by Mrs. Libnitz carrying the electric kettle. 'There's something I shall have to add to it. Can you hold it?'

'The hearing is tomorrow.'

'Let me have the carbon and I'll think about it while I'm out. I'll be back in the afternoon, four o'clock at the very latest. That will give you plenty of time, won't it?'

She went out of the room, leaving the carbon copy behind. I ran after her with it. Mrs. Libnitz had put a cup of coffee on my desk by the time I returned. She was sitting on the window seat looking into the garden. It seemed suddenly peaceful.

Mrs. Libnitz said, 'However you put up with them, I don't know.'

'Douglas says I am self-concerned.'

Mrs. Libnitz said something expressive in her own language. We drank our coffee. Doors opened and closed, feet descended the stairs. The side door opened and closed. I looked at my watch. It was half-past ten. Douglas was out visiting Mrs. Harrison and Di would not be in until this afternoon. Mrs. Libnitz and I sat in companionable silence. I could see the head and shoulders of a man on a tractor moving slowly above the hedgerows which bordered the lane. Beyond, in the far distance, were the chimneys of the Mill House. I had been there once as a child when old Mr. Leveridge had invited me to pick mulberries. He had taken me through the hall to the back door, pausing to speak to one of the maids while I looked at what I could see of the rooms on either side which were furnished quite differently to our house with couches and china cupboards and brass-framed mirrors. It had all seemed very handsome and hushed, bathed in a cool green light because one wall of the house was shaded by a vine. I wondered what the house was like now.

Mrs. Libnitz said, 'The snowdrops are out all around

the base of the tree.' Each year she was surprised by the English spring. There was a breeze blowing puffs of cloud across a pale blue sky and in the garden little tremors shook the leaves of the laurel.

A voice proclaimed dramatically, ' "*Oh, to be in England now that April's there!*" '

He was standing in the doorway, a short, square man with bright ginger hair and beard. He was wearing a striped blue suit with a hectic pink shirt and he reminded me of the buskers who used to entertain the queues at the county agricultural show. All he needed was a straw hat. Mrs. Libnitz eyed him with disfavour and said, 'This is March.'

'March House?' He struck a questioning pose; the music hall was obviously in his blood.

'The month of March.' Deadpan. She had no gift for crosstalk.

'And in England, I hope? "*Meadows of England in the rain/Open up your daisied lawns for me again* . . ." Is it daisy time yet? Perhaps not . . .' He held both hands out like a conjuror who has completed a trick. Mrs. Libnitz did not clap. He said, 'Try again. "*Daffodils that come before the swallow dares and take the winds of March with beauty*." How about that? Very appropriate, don't you think? Month of March . . . March House.' He looked at me. 'Have we daffodils?'

The proprietary 'we' took me by surprise. He was certainly not one of our clients. Perhaps he was one of the drug representatives? But March is a mad month and drug reps. are dull people; so I opted for madness and said, 'Dr. Laver, I presume.'

He looked at me as though I had asked more of him than that he be Dr. Laver and must myself make some comparable avowal. I said, 'I'm the clinic secretary.' He had very bright blue eyes which conveyed the impression that he already knew something about you and a naive

38

expectation that you would find this acceptable. I thought that he was a man who would make enemies without realising it. I said, 'You're not what I expected.'

He drew up a chair and sat close to me. 'What *did* you expect?' He asked the question as though the answer mattered. Whatever his gift for crosstalk, he appeared to have little understanding of small talk.

'I thought you'd be more my idea of a psychiatrist,' I answered, deliberately mundane.

'Do tell me what your idea is; I should so like to be what you desire.'

Mrs. Libnitz gave me a look which indicated that disapproval was in order. I rearranged the papers on my desk so that they were not facing him, in case this wasn't Dr. Laver at all but some lunatic at large, and said, 'Anxious and uptight, for a start.'

'It's important to run true to form?'

'Oh, very. Your backers aren't stable people; an unpredictable psychiatrist would bankrupt some of them.'

He reached out a hand and for a moment I thought he was going to pick up the case notes, but he said, 'FELT PENS!'

'I beg your pardon?'

'Do you mind?' He picked up my notebook and tore a sheet from it. 'I do so *love* felt pens. May I use this one? Can you draw Mickey Mouse? I remember a boy at school showing me. A half circle for each ear, then you join them with another larger one, then a curve. . . .' He was sketching a quite passable Mickey Mouse.

Mrs. Libnitz placed a cup of coffee on the desk in front of him and he acknowledged it earnestly. 'How enchanting! Thank you so much, that means you have accepted me.' He looked round the room. 'Well I suppose it's better than a haystack in a wet field. . . .'

Mrs. Libnitz returned to the switchboard, shutting the door firmly behind her. Dr. Laver winked at me.

Through the window I saw Iris walking towards the lane where her car was parked; Mrs. Haines was with her.

'That's our clinical psychologist,' I said. 'Shall I fetch her back?'

Dr. Laver went to the window and watched Iris opening the door of her car. 'Snow White or the Valkyrie?'

'The smaller of the two is Iris,' I replied, trying to preserve dignity. 'She is probably taking Mrs. Haines to the hospital because the bus service is so bad.'

'I don't think we should condemn poor Mrs. Haines to a long wait for the bus.'

'Iris will probably do visits in town. She may not be in again until tomorrow.'

'Then I can see her tomorrow.'

'Are we having you two days a week? Dr. Arnold only came once.'

'This place has a neglected look.' He swivelled round and surveyed the room like an actor in an empty auditorium. 'I feel it needs me. So, whatever happens subsequently, I *shall* come back tomorrow. Provided I don't die in the night, of course.'

'We shall be delighted.'

'Shall you? Does delight go with being anxious and — what was the other predictable quality — uptight?'

'We'd be glad of a little delight.'

'Well, we'll see what we can do about it.' His beard pointed in my direction. He reacted to the most casual utterance as though it was important which surprised me because in my experience psychiatrists are not very interested in people other than their clients. He said, 'Delight would not be impossible with that auburn hair and pale skin and although you seem a trifle muted at the moment there was earlier a brightness in your eyes.'

'I wasn't speaking personally. . . .'

He snapped his fingers. 'Of course you were speaking personally. How else do we speak?'

I dislike the personal, so I said, 'Well, I'd be delighted to be delighted. But I expect what you really want is to see some of the case files.'

He shrugged. 'If that is what you want.'

'We've got a stack of cases lined up for you.'

'What is your name, auburn-haired lady?'

'Ruth Saunders. Iris Bailey is our clinical psychologist and Douglas Gulliver is our psychiatric social worker. Di Brady is our nurse. They will be so relieved that you have come.'

'What do they expect that I will be able to do that they can't do?' He pointed a finger at me. 'You are blushing, Ruth Saunders! Tell me what you are thinking.'

'Iris doesn't expect you to do anything she can't do; neither does Douglas, but he would like the failure to be yours.' I had had no idea I was going to say this and was surprised to hear the words come out so boldly.

'So, when I see the clients there will be more of Douglas's because Iris will hold hers back?'

'No, you will see more of Iris's clients because she considers they are more important; and because Douglas feels guilty about wanting to get rid of his.'

'What does Di think?'

'It won't worry her either way.'

'And you? Who do you think I should see, Ruth?'

'How can I say?'

'False modesty. The clinic secretary always knows better than anyone else. Fetch the papers and tell me which eight clients you would take on your desert island. That way we shall cover the first month.'

'It won't be popular.'

'Nothing about the way I shall conduct this clinic will be popular.'

I laughed. There was something untoward about Dr. Laver to which I responded.

'Your face changes when you laugh. There is another, less careful person, that takes over. There now! She's gone. Why?'

'I don't want to be taken over by anyone.'

'Mmmh . . . Well, tell me about these. . . .' He flipped a finger up the side of the pile of papers I had produced.

He listened without intervening while I talked. When I had finished telling him about the cases, I saw that he had drawn up an appointments list for the coming weeks. The list was not one which would commend itself to either Iris or Douglas; and it was not the list which I would have drawn up if it had been left to me.

'Do you have a principle that you work on?' I asked, interested to know how these people came to find them-selves in the same company: autocratic old Mrs. Mapleton who disdainfully resisted all attempts to make life more tolerable for her; Josie Wilmer who forgot everything including her husband; Angus Brodie, the urbane, wife-beating civil servant; and Don Knight who fought for the rights of the workers but made his wife negotiate each week for her pay.

'Principles are very dull, don't you agree? I'm more effective if I'm interested — at least, I stay awake then. You look shocked. I suppose Iris and Douglas would be shocked, too? I always forget how seriously the lower orders take these matters.'

'The lower orders!' I thought of Iris who secretly believed that psychiatrists were redundant.

'Mrs. Brodie is too long-suffering to be credible, don't you think?' He was turning over the case notes. 'I wonder how she makes out in her dream life.'

This did not seem to call for comment.

'Do you talk with the clients while they are waiting, Ruth?'

'If they seem to want it.'

42

'I'm sure you are very good at it.' He looked at me in a way which I found disturbing; the eyes knew nothing of the reserves which govern most adult exchanges. He said, 'Perhaps you can introduce the subject of dreams. Tell Mrs. Brodie about your own.'

'I don't have dreams.'

He looked at me, his head to one side. 'I don't have dreams,' he mimicked. 'We don't have nasty things in our night life.'

'Nice or nasty, I don't have them.'

'*Someone* has them. Who is it, then, if it's not you, this other person you have around at night whom you won't acknowledge in the daytime?'

'I don't dream.' I was beginning to feel exhausted and it was all I could trust myself to say.

'Do you think you might manage to invent a dream or two to tell Mrs. Brodie?'

'No, I don't think so.'

'Doesn't dream, not inventive, very stubborn.'

This was too much. Tears came into my eyes. He was not embarrassed but observed me steadily. I have never cried in public before. For an appalling moment we gazed at each other and shared my crying. His eyes regarded me with an understanding unclouded by sentimentality. I found this unforgivable. Like most people, I wanted to be understood on my own terms, not unconditionally. He put his hands on my shoulders and said, 'Bless you, my child, there's nothing to be upset about; I'll soon have you dreaming nasty dreams like everyone else.'

I ran out of the room. In the cloakroom I cried for a little and then studied my face in the mirror. I had never been very concerned with my appearance and was not quite sure whether the present image of a pale, thin face with strained pink eyes did me justice or not. It didn't seem a promising subject for delight. There had

43

been a lot to do over the last few weeks and it must have tired me more than I had realised because it took several minutes for me to calm myself. When I came out of the cloakroom he was at the reception hatch talking to Mrs. Libnitz. He had found the invitation from Miss Maud and Mrs. Libnitz was telling him how to get to the Mill House. ' . . . or you can just walk across the fields. . . .'

I waited in the doorway to my room for Dr. Laver to return, but he picked up a small suitcase which he appeared to have left in the hall and went out of the main door. Mrs. Libnitz and I watched him turn into the lane where presumably he had left his car.

Mrs. Libnitz said, 'In England you have a saying, "mad as a March hare", yes?'

4

I T had been a hard winter and it was a particular joy to see the green shoots appearing, the leaves still clenched tight about the buds. Eleanor had come for the week-end to look through Mother's things to see whether there was anything she would like to keep. The garden tempted her, however, and she went out to help my father.

'You must tell me what to do,' she said, which pleased him.

Lethargy had seized me this week-end and it was an effort to move; so I sat on the grass with Punter and watched the two of them.

Eleanor wore a brown tweed skirt and a Fair Isle sweater; this was not her usual style, yet the garments had the look of being well-worn. Her shoes were sensible and she had gardening gloves which were undoubtedly new. It was apparent to me, if not to my father, that she had planned this week-end with the garden in mind.

'I worked so hard on the garden for Lillian,' my father said, resting a foot on his spade and looking down at the turned earth. He looked baffled. Yet when she was alive he had sought no explanation but seemed to accept their differences philosophically. It was she who became angry and made demands.

'Lillian was restless,' Eleanor said without looking up from her weeding. 'When she was in London she wanted to escape, and when she was in the country she wanted to get back to London.'

'I wondered sometimes if I had made a mistake coming

here.' He turned his head to look over the garden wall at the long view of fields and scattered trees. 'Whether it was too isolated . . .'

Eleanor sat back on her haunches, thinking; apparently she decided to offer no comfort for she picked up the trowel and absently uprooted a columbine without my father noticing.

'I may have been selfish,' he conceded tentatively, as though exploring a nerve to see if it would jump.

'I think you probably were,' Eleanor replied. 'But not more than most men.'

He began to dig again. 'It wasn't always easy for me, Eleanor.'

That was what Douglas had said to me about Charlotte, I thought. Eleanor took it in her stride. 'No,' she said, 'I don't suppose it was.'

'She had no idea of the pressure under which I work. I tried to make her understand that gardening was the only way I could relax. But I have been wondering lately whether I should have tried to get out a little more with her.' Eleanor came across another columbine and hesitated.

'That's a columbine, Eleanor,' I murmured. They are such graceful things, I could not bear to see them all savaged. She eased round and furtively extricated the uprooted columbine from the pile of weeds.

'But once you start that kind of thing in the country it tends to snowball,' my father said. 'You have to make a decision from the start whether to socialise or not.'

Eleanor replanted the columbine and pressed the earth around it with the flat of her gloved hand.

I wanted to stop my father talking about Mother. In the past when he had come home obviously tired after a day's work I had understood his longing to find peace and quiet at home and I had sympathised with him when Mother created tensions. But there was no need for him to defend himself in this way: it made his behaviour seem arguable.

'Miss Maud came into the office last week,' I said to change the conversation.

My father said, 'She sent a wreath, that was kind of her.'

'I didn't realise that. I don't think I've got her name on the list.'

Eleanor asked, 'Is she the dotty one who lives in the Mill House?'

'I don't know that she's dotty.' I felt a need to stand up for Miss Maud. 'She just lives the way she wants to.'

'To do that you have to be mad or rich,' Eleanor said bitterly.

'I don't think Miss Maud is rich. I think that one day she simply decided not to try to please people any more.'

'They were a bad family,' my father said. 'The old man was very harsh.'

'He let me pick the mulberries. I went into the house. I wonder what it's like now.' I was very interested although I had not given it a thought until recently. A picture of the hushed, old-fashioned room, shaded by the vine, came into my mind.

'I wouldn't talk to anyone but you like this, of course,' my father was saying to Eleanor. 'You were very close to her.'

Eleanor ran her hand slowly along her thigh. He was talking without giving thought to what he said, but she was thinking as carefully as though she was taking an oral examination. Eventually, she said, 'We weren't alike, Stewart.' She was very composed and even now, when she was wrecking the flower border, she had the air of being effective. But her plain, rather heavy face was not happy. On reflection, I didn't think I had ever seen Eleanor when she looked happy. She had always looked as though she was making the best of things. She had lived a different life to her sister's but seemed to have ended up as unsatisfied and less hopeful.

'You work,' my father said. 'So you understand what it's like to come home at night wanting to relax.'

'I have to come home at night and do the housework.'

'Oh? Mmmh. . . .' He frowned severely at the flower border. He seemed affronted that she should lay claim to problems of her own. 'Don't take up too many of the fox-gloves. I like to keep some of them.'

She sat looking down at a fat worm wriggling in the turned earth; she studied it as though she was completely absorbed by it, mind and body concentrated and disciplined.

My father walked along the border inspecting it. He said, 'For all I know you may be an excellent business woman, Eleanor; but you are no gardener.'

She stood up and brushed earth off her skirt. I think she was annoyed, because she had worked hard and deserved rather more than that; but she said pleasantly, 'How about a cup of tea?'

'Ah, now you are talking!'

When she had gone into the house he said to me, 'She hasn't the slightest idea what she's doing. Look at this!' He sounded pleased rather than annoyed.

After tea they worked in the garden until it was nearly dark and I took Punter for a walk. The Mill House was to the north of our house and some miles east of March House. I walked along a cart track to where there was a view of it across the flat fields. This did not please Punter who was very conservative and expected to be taken down to the river in the evening. There was one light on in a downstairs room in the Mill House. I wondered what Miss Maud did in the evening. It occurred to me that I should have thanked her for sending a wreath when I saw her at the clinic. Punter snuffled half-heartedly at rabbit holes and an old grey horse ambled across the field and put his head over the hedge; I rubbed his nose and he pressed against my hand, grateful for company. I wondered whether Dr. Laver would accept Miss Maud's invitation to a glass of wine next Wednesday. Punter pushed his head against my leg, agitated because he did not understand what we were doing here. I turned and walked him briskly in the direction of the river. Dr. Laver was going to make a difference to the clinic. Douglas had said he thought he would get things moving, and Iris had said he would be stimulating; but they had both seemed a little uneasy. I was uneasy, too. For years I had known exactly what to expect each day when I went into the office and although this was sometimes boring there was a comfort in the unvarying routine. There is much to be said for comfort.

When Punter and I came up the lane from the river my father was standing at the gate waiting for us. 'You were out a long time,' he said.

'You mustn't fuss me.'

'You'll have to bear with me. You are all I've got now.'

We went indoors. Eleanor had offered to cook the evening meal and we ate in the kitchen, the door open and the smell of turned earth and damp grass giving a feeling of satisfaction to the gardeners. Eleanor was a good cook and we enjoyed the meal. While she and I washed up my father talked about the Home Secretary, and the burden of working with a man who had so little grasp of the affairs of his Department; he talked about the problems created by the media and Lord Longford; about the incompetence of prison governors and the indulgence of prisoners. It was unusual for him to talk about his office. When we had finished washing up he said that we had all worked so hard he thought we should have brandy with our coffee. He seemed to want to please Eleanor and to put her in her place at the same time. When we were drinking our coffee, he said:

'What exactly is it you are doing now, Eleanor?'

'I'm personnel officer at the Armitage Life Assurance Company.'

'Really? That must be a very good job for a woman.'

'It was; but they have amalgamated with another company and the top personnel job has gone to a man who isn't even adequate, let alone able.'

He sipped his brandy. 'Of course, that is something I can't understand after all my years in the civil service where women are treated as equal to men.'

'How many permanent under-secretaries are women, Stewart?'

'I hope you're not a woman's libber?' He smiled at the absurdity of the idea. 'You wouldn't expect the Treasury, would you? Or the F.O.? Education, possibly . . . Social Security. . . .' Eleanor sipped her coffee. My father sighed and said, 'There is very little pleasure at the top, believe me, Eleanor.'

Eleanor put down her cup and studied the handle. 'Maybe you are right. At any rate, I've had enough.'

As I watched Eleanor it seemed to me that I was seeing someone slowly and laboriously remoulding their personality. I said impulsively, 'But you cared about it so much at one time, Eleanor.'

'She's older now, aren't you, Eleanor?' my father said, 'Older and wiser.'

Eleanor said, 'Older, certainly.'

'But wiser, too,' he insisted. 'There is nothing worse than a career woman; I was afraid you were going to become one at one time.' Eleanor raised her eyebrows. He went on, 'Women in authority become very hard. They can't take it, you see.'

Neither Eleanor nor I said anything.

'I can't understand why a woman can't be happy and content working at home. I would have thought most women would think themselves fortunate to avoid the pressures. I know my mother found it very creative to have a house and garden to look after.'

'She had servants,' I said.

'Only Dora now. And Mother spends more time looking after Dora than Dora spends looking after the house. But I suppose I'm old-fashioned. I just hope women know what they are doing, that's all. The ones I see in positions of authority don't give me the impression they are enjoying it very much.'

Eleanor had been studying his face while he talked; she looked at him not with sympathy or even with liking, but with a kind of application, just as I imagined her setting to work on a task at her office which was not congenial but which she had set herself to master.

'Do you think it has something to do with age?' she asked when my father had finished talking about how unhappy working women were. 'Perhaps it is only when people are older that they see things clearly? I sometimes think we spend the first half of our lives looking forward to some imagined goal and the second half looking backwards to see where we went wrong.'

She had changed the course of the conversation and my father and she began to talk elegiacally about the past. I left them to it as I found it depressing and went into the garden to see if any of the tools had been left lying about. Punter was out there, grieving for Mother. 'You must eat, Punter,' I told him. 'For my sake.' He pushed his face up into mine and licked my cheek. I remembered how as a child I had sat in the garden telling my troubles to the labrador, Jess, though I can't think what troubles I had then.

51

5

I HAD left school over twelve years ago. A lot had changed since then: extra buildings had been provided; many of the staff had left; next year, as a result of an amalgamation, boys were to be introduced. But the Head was still Miss Petrie. She must have been nearly sixty now, but seemed not to have altered since I was one of her more disappointing pupils; an austere woman with a tall, thin body surmounted by a tall, thin head, the hair scraped into a knot on top, giving the effect of a carving on a totem pole. I did not go back to the school unless I had to. Wednesday morning was one of the times when I had to; Iris had asked me to collect a report on one of the pupils which was needed that day for Dr. Laver's first clinic. The school was on Iris's route to the clinic, but she had said she could not afford the time to call. She was eager to see the clinic through from curtain rise. I felt the same and was aggrieved that she had not thought to mention the report the day before.

I took the car and instead of going the more familiar way, I did a detour through the country lanes which brought me out on the main road between Weston Market and Zetherney. The road had been widened and the lay-out changed; as I came up to the crossroads I thought: this is where I went wrong last time. I turned towards Zetherney because the view was so much more attractive that way. Ten minutes later, on my way back, I thought dismally: I always remember that I went wrong before, but I never learn from it, and the next time round I do the wrong thing again — this is the story of my life.

I realised as I approached the school that it was not the irritation of having to fetch the report which was disturbing me, it was something deeper than that. I parked the car in the yard near the kitchen and wound the window down. I felt reluctant to get out.

I had not been unhappy at the school. So why should I be so loth to revisit it? Admittedly, a lot had been expected of one; but, even though I personally had not come up to expectations, I was prepared to acknowledge that the school had done well by most of its pupils. I myself had not suffered unduly; no one had been unkind to me because I had failed to achieve. Now, as I sat and looked at the building, I did not feel bitter or resentful. But I did feel very tired, as though I was coming to the end of something that had been going on for a long time.

While I was sitting there, the familiar feeling came over me that someone was standing just behind me, noticing some sin of omission or commission of which I was unaware but would soon be made aware. There was a strong sense of unseen, pervading disapproval that seemed to rise from the asphalt. Perhaps there had been a notice at the entrance gates saying that cars were not to be parked in the yard today because there was a governors' meeting?

I got out of the car; but I did not go back to the entrance gates to see if there was such a notice. I had broken rules before and if necessary would do so again today. I went through the door at the side of the main block. The secretary's room was opposite the entrance. The secretary was typing the report for Iris; she looked hot and flustered and said I would have to wait. I could see that it was more than she could bear to have the Head waiting in her study for the report and me breathing down her neck while she typed it, so I said that I would take a stroll. 'As you know, I'm an old girl . . .' I left the remark hanging, suggesting a nostalgia for old times which I did not feel. In fact, I was glad to escape from the room because I was afraid Miss Petrie might come in and take me off to her room for a talk. It was known that Miss Petrie always made time to see old girls when they visited the school.

In the corridor I felt, if anything, rather worse. There was a buzz of distant, controlled activity: whistle blasts from the games' field; the sound of a phrase repeated constantly from the music-room; nearer at hand a young voice reading French with constant corrections of pronunciation. It was just as I remembered it, all stops and starts, mistakes and corrections, trying again . . .

'You can't say *The Pot of Basil* is rubbish, Ruth. You can say Tennyson is rubbish if you like, but not Keats.'

Subsequently, I had written an essay about an aboriginal who came fresh to the English cultural scene; but it had not been a success because I could not think like an aboriginal. The realisation that I could not switch off all the ideas which were being fed into me had shaken me more than the teacher's 'try something a little less ambitious next time'. I had had a nightmare vision of myself as a pillar-box, mouth helplessly open, into which other people's mail was being stuffed so that soon there would be no room for anything addressed to me.

Now, standing in the corridor, I had the same feeling of suffocation that I had had then. I opened the outer door and went into the playground. But when I was half-way across the playground the flat expanse began to bother me and I felt I was losing my balance. The side door opened and girls began to stream out on to the playground. I had to make my way between them, absurdly panicky because the feeling of loss of balance persisted and I was afraid I would bump into one of them. I regained the corridor and found the secretary waiting for me.

'I wondered where you had gone,' she said crossly.

'Miss Petrie would like to see you.'

Before I could protest she opened the door to the Head's room and held it for me; there was no escape. I went in. Miss Petrie was waiting to greet me, not formally, on the far side of her desk, but coming towards me, hands outstretched.

'My dear Ruth, I heard about your mother; I am so sorry!' To my surprise she spoke with deep feeling as though reliving a grief in her own past.

I said, 'Oh, I'm quite all right,' my voice high and unconvincing even to me.

She looked at me and nodded her head, accepting something I had not known was in need of acceptance. Then, with what I recognised as innate sensitivity (a quality I had not perceived in her before) she began to talk of other things.

'And how is the clinic managing? I heard you were without a psychiatrist.'

'We have one as from last week.'

'That must make a great difference?' Half-querying, deferring without condescension to my greater knowledge of these matters. We talked for a time of the clinic and its work. She was interested to know how it differed from the clinics run by the County. Did we, for example, have the same trouble getting people to attend regularly, or did they cherish us more because they had to pay for our services?

'They don't all have to pay,' I said. 'We have our version of the "assisted places" scheme.'

'But you are not dependent on the whim of government for your grant?'

'The Foundation can be fairly whimsical.'

All the time we were talking I was aware of her gaze on me, not analytical as Iris's so often was, but sad. I could not tell whether the sadness was something new in her or occasioned by me.

55

'Do you come across the Cooper family?' she asked.

'I've heard of them, of course; but they don't come our way.'

'We have three of the girls with us now. The family lives in a caravan down by the river at present. Very happy-go-lucky people. I have to get the education welfare officer to chase them, and if we are all very severe they attend regularly for a few months. The summer is the worst time. On a sunny day Mrs. Cooper keeps them at home.' She looked out of the window; her room, no doubt sited as far as possible from the playground, faced north-east. 'Sometimes when I am sitting here I can imagine them all playing like gypsies and I wonder which of us has got our priorities right.'

'The education office would give you the answer to that.'

'Yet I feel perhaps we should be able to accommodate children like the Coopers better than we do.'

She smiled ruefully. I had the impression that an offering of a kind was being made, not only to the Coopers and their alien values. Out in the corridor there was the sound of scampering feet and a voice raised in admonition. I said that I must get back to the clinic with the report.

'You like your work at the clinic?' she asked, rising.

'It's near home,' I said, without thinking, just something to say.

She nodded her head as though I had confirmed what was in her mind. After a pause she said diffidently, 'I know how fond you are of your home; but do you suppose one day you may feel you want to branch out a little?'

'I've never regretted not going to university,' I said defensively.

'I wasn't thinking of that.' She spoke as though the idea was irrelevant now. 'It was wrong to have made an issue of that; there were too many pressures on you.'

'I don't remember any, only the university thing.'

She looked out of the window again, meditating; I found that my heart was thudding. Whatever was in her mind, she decided not to put it into words.

'I mustn't keep you now, Ruth. I hope I may see you another time, though.' It was there again, that suggestion of accepting something about me that had nothing to do with my academic record.

It was a relief, on coming into the yard, to find that my car had blocked the passage of a delivery van. The care-taker was waiting for me. 'I thought it was you,' he said. 'I called out to you when you drove in, but you didn't take any notice.' I apologised and he said, 'Get on with you, you're not really sorry! You always were a naughty girl.' I was happier with this verdict than with Miss Petrie's.

Iris had asked me to call at the social services depart-ment offices in Weston Market and I wasted a lot of time there waiting for a social worker who, it transpired, was in court that day. It was a quarter to one when I returned to March House and I imagined that I would have missed the whole of the morning session. As I came in the front door I realised, however, that this was not so; it seemed I had arrived in time for the final scene. The participants were off-stage, but the door of the room used by the psy-chiatrist must have been open and I could hear Angus Brodie's voice raised in complaint. Other sounds came to my ear, a low, soothing murmur from Iris, Douglas's nervous cough, and a fantastic orchestration of keening and yodelling which must emanate from Mrs. Brodie. Our clinic sessions did not usually end like this. I could see Mrs. Libnitz's head and shoulders framed in the re-ception hatch looking as disorientated as a traveller in a space capsule who has come across an unknown galaxy.

Dr. Laver's voice, robustly good-humoured, inter-rupted Mr. Brodie. 'What's this? Your wife was serviced

only last month and she's gone wrong already? My dear
sir, I'll give her another overhaul and there'll be no
charge. And while we're about it, why not have a check
on the rest of the family? Any trouble with your son and
daughter? Bring them along; I'll throw them in for
nothing. Can't have dissatisfied customers at this clinic.
What about you? Hand a bit unsteady, eyes bloodshot,
been at the bottle lately? How about another liver while
we're on the job? You're going to need one soon by the
look of you.' It was like a knock-about musical hall turn
with up-dated patter.

Steps sounded on the stairs. Mrs. Libnitz abandoned
the switchboard and disappeared into the stationery
store; Mrs. Brodie ran into the ladies' cloakroom
followed by Iris; and I darted into my room and looked
round frantically for something which would indicate
that I was so occupied that on no account could I be
interrupted however great the emergency. The door
opened and Mr. Brodie came in. In this rather
frightening game, I was the one who had run in the
wrong direction and must now pay the penalty. I looked
warily at Mr. Brodie. After Dr. Laver's contribution,
anything seemed possible.

Mr. Brodie at this moment looked like one of the more
despotic Roman emperors in modern dress. The frill of
curly hair stood up like a crown of leaves around his
balding scalp, the long straight nose flared at the nostrils
and the imperious mouth twisted in something that was
mid-way between snarl and smile. He looked like a man
sated with experience who has miraculously found a new
happening to savour. One could almost believe, looking
at him, that it was within the power of a very senior civil
servant to demand of his minister the head of an
offending psychiatrist on a charger.

In the hope of introducing a little normality into the
proceedings, I said, 'Good afternoon, Mr. Brodie; did

58

you want to fix your next appointment?'

The door of the room had opened as I said this, and Iris had entered. She rolled her eyes to the ceiling and shook her head at me; but I had now committed myself to my line of defence and I pretended to consult the diary. Mr. Brodie came and stood beside me; he smelt of gin. I said, 'Six weeks? Is ten o'clock a good time for you?'

Mr. Brodie's eyes opened very wide; they were expressive eyes which on this occasion seemed over-charged with conflicting emotions, astonishment, out-rage, contempt and an inappropriate merriment making it difficult to assess his reaction. He looked at the diary and his eyes moved over its unexceptional surface as though it fascinated him and he wanted to possess it. He bared his teeth and sucked in air. Some kind of a struggle seemed to be going on inside him. Iris was observing him with interest. Mr. Brodie said, 'In view of what I and my wife have just been subjected to, we can hardly be expected to wait another six weeks. You will give us an appointment in three weeks' time, please.'

I gave him an appointment for April the seventh. He made a note of it, bade us both a courteous good-day and went out of the room. Iris crossed to the window and watched until he left the building accompanied by his wife; then she turned to me. 'Well, well, that was very instructive. You could see him struggling with the know-ledge that he ought to make a fuss, couldn't you?'

'I can't understand why he didn't.'

'There was something about the session this morning that was irresistible to him; he *had* to come again. Dr. Laver is very clever, of course; but I think he took a risk.'

Before she could say any more, Douglas and Di came in. Douglas said to me, 'Who have we got this afternoon?'

'Josie Wilmer.'

'Thank goodness for that! We aren't likely to have fireworks there.'

Di said, 'A pity!'

Douglas said shortly, 'Don't be silly.' He turned to Iris. 'Come and have a word with me in my room.'

'I seem to have missed quite a session,' I said to Di when they had gone.

'He was great. This place needs a dose of salts!'

'Iris thinks Mr. Brodie found it irresistible, a new experience that he can't pass up.'

'Yeah?'

'Do you know, Di, coming in at the end like that, quite cold, I got a different impression.'

She raised her eyebrows.

'I had the feeling he was trying to get rid of them, behaving so absurdly that they wouldn't come back.'

'He didn't succeed then, did he?'

'No, because I think Mr. Brodie had the same idea, and he wasn't going to play.'

Di shrugged her shoulders. 'Doesn't seem likely, does it? What would he do for clients?'

I didn't have an answer to that.

'I'll tell you one thing,' Di said. 'Things aren't going to be run Iris's way any longer. There's going to be a real ding-dong. You should have seen her face when she came out after that session.'

'I can't say that I blame her. I don't want everything to be upheaved.'

'Come on, Ruth! Anything's better than the way things have been lately.'

Her days were disconnected events; as long as she wasn't bored she did not ask what the events were leading up to. To her Dr. Laver's advent was in the same category as an unexpected week-end abroad or an evening ride to London in a fast car; it was all experience, and all experience was good provided it didn't go on so long it became routine.

'One of the kids has chicken pox,' she said. 'I promised

him I'd go home at lunch-time.'

'Is your mother with him?'

'Yes. I rang her up at eight this morning, She wasn't very pleased. She hasn't had chicken pox.'

When she had gone it was quiet for a few minutes, then the telephone buzzed. It was Dr. Laver. 'I thought you had run away. Come in and explain yourself. And bring your sandwiches and your notebook. We're going to have a working lunch.'

'Iris and Douglas will expect to join us.'

'I have already dealt with that expectation. You do your job and I'll do mine and then we'll get along very nicely.' He put down the receiver. There seemed to be no alternative but to join him.

The psychiatrist's room was on the first floor. It was a large room with a view over the garden and it had been decorated in silver grey and furnished with chairs and a small settee upholstered in pale lemon ribcord. Every effort had been made to create an atmosphere that was informal and unalarming; even the pictures had been chosen with care. In spite of this, it usually had a dull, static quality like a bad painting which was vaguely depressing. Things were different today. My first thought on entering the room was that the painstaking effort expended on choosing pictures which were not distracting would hardly seem to have been worthwhile if the psychiatrist himself was to be so gaudy. He was wearing the same striped suit and pink shirt which, perhaps combined with something left hovering in the air from the morning's jamboree, gave to the room a feeling of unrest. It was an atmosphere in which Dr. Laver appeared to thrive. He was laying out food on the occasional table near the window: a loaf of bread, a jar of pickles, a generous portion of brie, an apple, a tray of peanuts, a bar of chocolate, and a bottle of tonic water. He arranged these items with what seemed rather obsessional care. There was a pile of disordered papers on the floor.

'I had a drink problem at one time,' he said. 'They told me that whenever I wanted a drink I should have tonic water; now I'm addicted to the stuff.' He tipped peanuts into his cupped hand.

I put my cheese and biscuits and two tomatoes on the occasional table. He downed his peanuts and said incredulously, 'Is that all you have?'

'I never feel hungry mid-day.'

'It's bad for you to eat so little, no wonder you are thin.'

'I eat a big supper,' I said.

He stuffed a hunk of bread and cheese in his mouth. 'You've got a nice enough little face at the moment; but in a few years you'll be haggard.'

'I take after my father.'

'Does Daddy run away from dreams, too?'

I balanced a piece of cheese carefully on a biscuit. 'I'm sorry I wasn't in this morning; Iris wanted me to fetch a report . . .'

'I'm afraid you haven't escaped the dream world. We will be making notes of Mrs. Brodie's dreams. Do you think you can bring yourself to do that?'

'Are they important?'

'You heard Mr. Brodie; he seemed to think so.'

'It was your reply that I heard. Aren't you taking a risk, treating them like that?'

'Yes, of course. What do you think this business is about? Anyone who comes to a psychiatrist and imagines they aren't risking themselves is very unwise.'

'But Mr. and Mrs. Brodie seemed *so* upset. Aren't we supposed to be trying to reconcile them?'

'Mightn't it be wiser to put them asunder? They have been together for over twenty years without any sign of becoming reconciled to each other.'

'I feel sorry for Mrs. Brodie. She's the one who will suffer if they are torn asunder.'

'I said "put asunder" and you say "torn asunder". How interesting! Did you bring your notebook as well as those disgusting scraps you are nibbling? Now: this is dream one.

'A man is coming into a house. She watches him and she knows something terrible is going to happen. Yet she cannot warn him. In the house there are two children. They are in the basement. The man must not go into the basement where the children are. One of the children is retarded. As she looks at the child, it seems to become less and less human and more like a lumpish piece of sculpture, something unfinished, embryonic. It is this crude thing which threatens the man. The man goes to the cellar door. The other child, who is not very pleasant but is still recognisably formed, tries to hold back its ill-fashioned companion; but as the man goes down the cellar steps the thing begins to jig about wildly. She knows that the thing will tear the man apart. It is so horrible that she wakes up.'

While he was dictating this he had consumed the brie. He ate quickly and greedily, but this did not prevent him from watching every outline that I made. I wondered if he could read shorthand, or whether it was just that he must always give this impression of immense interest in what other people were doing.

'In dream two, she is a child in a house with her mother and her grandmother, and a man is holding them up with a gun. She manages to escape through a skylight, but when she is outside she sees that the house is being watched by policemen and she knows she will not be able to get away without the policemen seeing her, so she goes back to the house.'

There was silence while I finished making notes. Dr. Laver poured himself a glass of tonic water. 'Are you sure now that it is Mrs. Brodie who will suffer if they are "torn" asunder?'

'Poor Mrs. Brodie! How she must be wishing she had never come out with that dream about the children!'

'An ominous dream, certainly.'

'It was beastly.'

'But it was Mrs. Brodie who dreamt every beastly detail of it.'

'Yes, I know all about that; but I think it's unhealthy to probe these things.'

'Mrs. Brodie doesn't come to the clinic because she is in the best of health.' He unwrapped the chocolate, tearing impatiently at the silver paper so that he got chocolate in his nails. 'And the other dream. What did you make of that?'

'I don't want to make anything of it. What good can it have done her to tell you these dreams?'

'There are destructive forces in everyone, Ruth; even in you. Particularly in you, who are so unvaryingly quiet and reasonable. What is it you are angry about?'

I laughed because now he was being predictable. 'That's a bit of psychiatric one-up-manship I'm hardly likely to fall for after three years in this place! If you want to put your opponent out of countenance ask "What do you do with your anger?" '

He broke off several squares of chocolate and put them in his mouth. He watched me as he ate. 'Why did you call me your opponent? In spite of the calm reasonableness we have been noting in you, your choice of words is sometimes unexpectedly aggressive.'

'You have been getting at me ever since I came into the room. *I* call *that* aggressive.'

'How very well-defended you are.'

'Oh no, not *that*!'

'Yes, you are right to be scornful.' He licked his fingers. 'These phrases have not worn well. Yet psychology is comparatively young; there can seldom have been a language which has grown stale so quickly. That is why we have to find some other way of experiencing the truth about ourselves.'

'We are back with dreams, are we?'

'Not only dreams.' I waited but he turned away and began to peel an apple. 'You can go now. I shall have a little sleep in a minute or two.'

I collected my papers, balanced my food container on top of them, and left the room. It was half-past one. Mrs. Wilmer was due to arrive at two-fifteen. Douglas and Iris were waiting in my room. Iris was seething and the seething was expressed in her body, clearly outlined beneath a tight-fitting black jumper and wine-red skirt: storm signals went out from the swell of breasts, the thrust of hips. Douglas had retired to the far corner. He was dressed in a charcoal-grey suit with a silver-grey polo necked sweater which seemed designed to shade into the background.

Iris said to me, 'I think I'll have a talk with Dr. Laver now about one or two general matters.'

'I don't think he wants to be disturbed.'

'Why not? Everyone else has been.'

'He's eating.'

'Eating!' She expected that while the psychiatrist was on the premises he would devote every minute to work. Dr. Arnold had been driven to spending long periods in the lavatory to escape from Iris.

'He also said something about sleeping.'

'I've never heard such nonsense.'

'Churchill used to sleep at odd times during the day,' I consoled her. 'Dr. Laver will probably wake like a lion refreshed.'

This proved not to be the case. When I went in at ten-past two to tell him that Mrs. Wilmer had arrived he was still asleep in the armchair and barely raised his head when I wakened him.

c

'If she's so forgetful, how does she manage to arrive five minutes early?' he asked crossly.

'She comes by taxi.'

'How does she remember the taxi?'

'Perhaps you can ask her that.'

'I'm not going to see people who come early.'

I assumed there was no need to reply to this and occupied myself straightening the room which had acquired a stale, crumpled appearance and smelt of cheese and pickles.

'Tell her to go away,' he said.

'Do you want to fetch her, or shall I bring her to you? She won't make it on her own.'

He closed his eyes. 'I am not going to see this woman.'

I went out of the room and collected Mrs. Wilmer. It was not until I had opened the door of his room, and seen him standing waiting to receive her, that I acknowledged that I had had some nasty doubts in my mind.

'Does he want me or Douglas to join him later on?' Iris asked. She was pacing the corridor, angered by what she considered to be cavalier treatment.

'I expect he'll tell you,' I said. 'Perhaps we ought to play it his way for today, Iris?'

'I was hoping for your sake that we were going to have some joint sessions,' she said to Douglas. 'It would be such a help to you, wouldn't it?'

'Not if they are like this morning's session.' Douglas was annoyed. It was all very well for a psychiatrist to use shock tactics on a client; he did not have to pick up the pieces afterwards. Douglas was not looking forward to his next visit to Mr. and Mrs. Brodie. 'At this rate I shall wish we had old Arnold back.'

'Arnold was a nonentity,' Iris said.

'I'd rather work with a nonentity than a whizz kid,' Douglas replied crossly.

Iris said, 'Oh come, we mustn't make judgements.'

Mrs. Wilmer left at half-past three looking as quietly disorientated as she had when she arrived. She was one of the more perplexing cases and Iris and Douglas were eager to discuss her with Dr. Laver. Iris tutted with impatience when he demanded a break for tea. 'I think we'll join him now,' she said, and led the way up to his room.

I did not enjoy being present at case conferences and when I brought in their tea I tried to excuse myself on the grounds that there was so much work to do. Dr. Laver, however, was insistent and Iris supported him. 'We may have to implement new procedures. You must be in on this from the start, Ruth. You know how much we all depend on you.'

I handed round the tea cups and then sat beside Dr. Laver. Douglas and Iris were doing most of the talking. This was their first opportunity to tell him about the work of the clinic and they intended to make the most of it. The point which they were both trying to put across was that the psychiatrist did his sessions and departed leaving to them the real business of supporting the clients. They, in their turn, had need of support. This had never been acknowledged by Dr. Arnold and they were concerned that Dr. Laver should be left in no doubt about it right from the start. To Douglas it was a straightforward question of needing help; to Iris, the issue was more complicated, since she would not brook too much interference but did not want to be left out of the supportive circle.

Dr. Laver listened intently, gazing first at Douglas, then at Iris, with that strange mixture of naiveté and understanding I had noted in him before. It was like seeing an immensely knowing child watching the performance of a well-known play for the first time. One's own reaction has been conditioned by previous productions and many reviews; but the child is able to enter totally into what is taking place on stage. The reactions are immediate, but, to the jaded viewer, seem totally inappropriate. Although Dr. Laver was entering into this so completely, he was not involved emotionally, was not necessarily sympathetic. He is my aboriginal! I thought suddenly.

Douglas and Iris seemed unaware of all this; in fact, they were not very aware of Dr. Laver. They were pre-occupied with themselves. Now they were discussing Mrs. Wilmer, ostensibly for Dr. Laver's benefit, but in reality pursuing their never-ending attempt to stake out their own particular piece of clinical territory.

Douglas said, 'Mrs. Wilmer forgets because she can't face up to life. She doesn't want to wash the dishes, so she forgets they are there.'

'There is an element of convenience, no doubt.' Iris was dismissive. She always treated other people's opinions as a threat to be put down without delay. 'A method of getting her own way, perhaps. A form of aggression? All of that. Something else, though.' She shook her head, implying deep, but incommunicable knowledge which could not possibly be shared with a social worker. 'Difficult, very difficult.'

There was a pause. Douglas said, 'A poor self-image . . .'

'I'm not even sure about that.' Iris came in quickly to put down this pretension. 'A refusal to conform to the mores of her society; a secret pride in herself . . .'

Douglas, usually lazy, for once seemed unprepared to be out-talked. He applied himself to the problem and said, 'She has retreated into a little room in her own skull and thrown away the key.' Iris was intensely surprised by this rather literary statement. He said defensively, 'Well, that's the effect she has on me, anyway.'

'In which case, what are we supposed to do?' Dr. Laver asked. 'We don't know what goes on in that little world; it may be richer than anything we imagine. Are we justified in breaking in?'

'Surely she is very near a state of complete breakdown.' Iris was indulgent.

'And?' He looked at her, pulling at his beard; then he swivelled round in his chair and sat with his back to the room looking out into the garden. Iris and Douglas each studied a different part of the room. I had that panic-stricken feeling one has in a theatre when an actor dries up and players and audience are left stranded between the real and the unreal world. Someone had to say something. I said, 'How can you say that we should abandon poor Mrs. Wilmer?'

'No one is suggesting we should abandon Mrs. Wilmer, Ruth,' Iris said reprovingly. I was not expected to speak at these meetings, except to ask when they wanted tea.

'You and Douglas have been talking of nothing else for months!'

'All that I have ever said was that I didn't feel she was a suitable case for this clinic.'

'And Douglas thinks he isn't the person who should be dealing with her. And now Dr. Laver says we aren't justified in doing anything because we don't know what goes on in her mind. I call that abandoning her.'

Iris tucked in her chin and regarded me judicially.

Douglas said, 'It's quite true, I don't think I should be dealing with her. I've said so ever since Arnold left.' He looked accusingly at Iris.

'I have a very long waiting list.'

'Social workers, alas, don't have waiting lists.'

Dr. Laver said, 'I didn't get far with Mrs. Wilmer, either.' He swivelled back into view. The relief in the room was almost tangible; God was back in business again.

Iris said, 'Your first clinic! It must have been such an exhausting day for you. We're all being terribly selfish.'

She managed to sound solicitous while conveying the message that psychiatrists could scarcely be expected to cope with the burdens which clinical psychologists shouldered daily. She walked across the room and picked up the teapot. While they drank their tea, Iris said gracefully to Douglas that she knew she should have taken Mrs. Wilmer's case after Dr. Arnold left, and Douglas, who could be graceless, said perhaps she would take it over now. Dr. Laver, who was doing a complicated abstract design on his copy of the case history, said, 'There is one way of approaching Mrs. Wilmer's problem which hasn't been tried.'

'Do tell us.' Douglas spoke with quiet sarcasm.

Dr. Laver added a flourish to his design. 'Mrs. Wilmer can tell us herself.'

Douglas put his cup and saucer down carefully on the floor, then took out his handkerchief and polished his glasses; Iris smiled wisely to herself. The silence was prolonged. Dr. Laver showed no inclination to enlarge on his statement but continued to embellish his design.

Iris, aware that Douglas had no intention of taking Dr. Laver to task, asked, 'Are we talking about dreams, again?'

'No, I pursued that with Mrs. Wilmer, but she is not a good subject.' He did a great curlicue across the top of the sheet.

Iris said, 'Ah.' She and Douglas were relieved, but a trifle disappointed. This morning's experience, viewed in the light of the afternoon session, seemed to have gained in attraction.

Dr. Laver put his beard close to the paper, lower lip jutting out while he executed some delicate scrollwork. 'I can see there is a certain resistance to new techniques, so I am reluctant to make a suggestion.'

Douglas, being wary, was prepared to suffer this accusation in silence, but Iris said, 'I *hope* we are not resistant to new techniques. It depends what one regards as new, I suppose; the analysis of dreams could hardly be described as a new technique, could it?'

'Perhaps I am wrong.' Dr. Laver sat up and pushed the drawing aside. 'Before I try a new treatment on Mrs. Wilmer I should like to talk it over with you so that you can think about it before we reach a final decision. Any decision taken should, I think, be a team decision.'

They brightened at the prospect of being a team again.

'What had you in mind?' Iris took upon herself the role of spokesman.

'Hypnotism.'

'Hypnotism!' Iris ran the clinic; it was her arena. She was about as pleased by this suggestion as a Cleopatra might have been to see Isis doing the dance of the seven veils as she clasps the asp to her bosom.

'You have objections?' Dr. Laver gazed at Iris's breasts which had swelled superbly.

'Do you imagine . . . Have you any idea of the difficulty of getting people to attend, voluntarily, a clinic of this kind? They may be used to watching TV programmes about psychiatry; they may be familiar with the more publicised techniques and have a superficial knowledge of the jargon; but this is something which is happening to other people. The vast majority of ordinary people are still very resistant to psychiatry happening to them. It is hard enough as it is for G.P.s to persuade their patients to come here; but to tell them that when they arrive they will be hypnotised by the psychiatrist . . .' She put her head back and gave a laugh which fell a fraction short of delight. 'You would have to start by converting the G.P.s.'

'It has been done.'

'But not here! It may be all right with trendy medicos in London, but it certainly wouldn't go down here in the sticks.'

Dr. Laver regarded Iris with bright, unblinking eyes. He was quite as intent on winning as she was and yet there was something one-sided about the confrontation. It occurred to me that while Iris was summoning her resources to the fray, Dr. Laver did not see himself as engaged with her. The possibility of defeat was something he did not admit. Such inflexibility in a mature person is a little chilling. After a moment, he said, 'How familiar are the G.P.s with the current situation in this clinic?'

The choice of the words 'this clinic' suggested a place where something questionable had happened. There was an awkward silence. He looked down, fingering the list of 'current' cases which had been prepared for him. Earlier in the week he had asked me to write beside the name of each client the date of the last visit to the clinic. Many of the people on the list had not been seen for a considerable time. 'Does the Foundation know how low the numbers are?' he had asked me.

Now he asked, 'What does "R" stand for?'

Iris looked at me expectantly, but I decided she could handle this. She said, 'Residential.'

'But we have no residential clients at present?'

'No.'

He nodded his head and began ostentatiously to make a tally, ticking the number of genuinely current cases. Douglas cleared his throat.

'I should be quite prepared to move out if Iris and her family would like to take over.'

'I don't see why Eddie can't move out,' Iris said sharply. 'In fact, he scarcely seems to be here. I never see him.'

'I seldom see your family,' Douglas said. 'But I assume them to exist.'

Iris was startled by this rapid return of fire. Although she was ready to admit to being 'a typical Aries'

72

—dominating and assertive and, therefore, at times difficult to work with—she did not see herself as being the
object of real animosity. Now, perhaps beginning to feel
herself in danger of isolation, she addressed Dr. Laver in
a more conciliatory manner. 'You have a lot of
experience in this particular field?'

'I suppose you might say that.' It was not in him to be
conciliatory.

'And you find the results encouraging?' she persisted.

He rubbed his nose. 'They encourage me; I don't know
about the subjects.'

Iris said coldly, 'Perhaps I didn't word that very well. It
is your experience that a not inconsiderable number of
people can be helped by hypnosis when other treatments
have failed?'

'I think you still haven't worded it very well. What, for
example, would you regard as a not inconsiderable
number? Don't bother to answer. Statistics won't carry
any conviction.'

'But would you agree that other methods should be
tried first?'

'Such as?'

'Joint counselling sessions with the family have often
proved very successful here.' Iris had in the past played
the dominant role in such sessions.

Dr. Laver said, 'I find I succeed with hypnosis when I
have failed with other treatments.'

Iris pondered this, eyeing Dr. Laver speculatively as
though assessing whether this admission was indicative of
genius, humility, or a failed psychiatrist. Douglas flexed
his hands and examined his knuckles unhappily; no
doubt he was torn between his dislike of the suggestion
and his fear of having his changed domestic affairs
brought to the notice of the Foundation. He said,
'Perhaps we could have a discussion about this another
time?'

'We could have a mild experiment among ourselves, if you like, before practising on the clients.' Dr. Laver spoke casually, but he was not master of the throw-away line and it was apparent to me that the whole discussion had been leading up to this moment.

'You mean you would hypnotise one of *us*?' Iris asked.

'All of you might be better.' Casual again, examining his finger nails. 'It would avoid any one person feeling awkward about it.'

Iris and Douglas looked at each other. They might have done better, I felt, to study him.

He said, 'You need have no fear. There are constraints which apply even under hypnosis. Nothing will be dragged from you against your will; all that can happen is that those things which are asking for attention may receive your attention.'

This did not appear to reassure Iris and Douglas. I began to collect my papers.

'I wonder if you would give us some idea of what might be involved?' Iris asked pleasantly: she was good at dealing with other people's ideas.

'Indeed, when you have decided whether or not you wish to proceed with the suggestion.'

'But if we could have some idea . . .'

'I don't find this trade in ideas very constructive. How can I give you an idea of what it is like to be under hypnosis? It is something to be experienced. If you do not experience it, how can you make a decision as to whether it is a suitable form of treatment for your clients?'

'I have never been a patient in a psychiatric ward,' Iris pointed out. 'Should that preclude me from being a party to recommending such treatment?'

'Ah, now that is something we might well discuss.' He sounded almost genial. 'But I think you are evading the present issue which is whether hypnosis is a suitable treatment for our clients.'

Iris frowned; the form of treatment was, finally, a decision for the psychiatrist to take, but if she said this she might seem to be giving her blessing to the proposal. On the other hand, if she rejected it, she would be assuming a responsibility which should not have been hers. Since Dr. Arnold left she had assumed a good deal of responsibility which should not have been hers. Dr. Laver had hinted as much. Her eyes moved from side to side as she backtracked over the discussion to see how she had arrived at this point. She was thinking of herself. I wanted to tell her: Take a look at this man; think about *him* before you commit yourself! Iris said, 'I think this should be a joint decision. I agree with Douglas that we should talk about it another time.'

At least she had won time for reflection.

Dr. Laver said, 'You are very quiet, Ruth.'

'There is a lot of work to be done before I go home. Do you mind if I leave you now?'

'You will be involved in this, Ruth. You are part of the team.'

'I can give you my answer now.'

'That is why I am not asking for it now.'

I made for the door; before I reached it, he said, 'There is one other matter I want to mention while we are all here. I have been looking at these case files and I find the language uncongenial. I should like our reports to be written without the use of such words as "supportive", "sharing" and this terrible marriage of piety and technology — "caring input".'

Douglas, who found great difficulty in writing his reports, protested, 'I can't possibly do that! What words can I use?'

'There are other words.'

'I haven't the time to sit down and think about "other words".' A fly had been buzzing round the room for some time; Douglas was now agitated by it and he got up and opened the window.

'That is exactly how these reports read,' Dr. Laver went on relentlessly, oblivious of distractions. 'They read as though you hadn't had time to think so you have used a convenience language.'

'Do you know how many reports we have to do a week?' Iris asked.

Douglas leant out of the window, arms resting on the sill. Unfortunately, it was the window which had a broken sash cord; we had all been warned that it was dangerous. Douglas had time to take one good gulp of air before it descended knocking him forward and pinning him by the shoulder blades. His glasses fell into the garden below which seemed to distress him more than anything else. Iris and I ran to the window. Dr. Laver followed us, but only to continue the argument.

'I can imagine how many reports *should* be done a week, but in fact this is the only one I have seen.'

Iris and I tugged at the window but could not raise it. On the other side of the glass Douglas groaned, 'My glasses, oh my glasses!'

Iris said breathlessly, 'In any case, the recipients wouldn't understand if we used other words . . . '

'You mean their minds are set to receive this language and this language only?'

'From another professional, yes. Oh dear, we aren't going to be able to manage this, Ruth; it's jammed.'

Dr. Laver said loudly, 'Well, I demand another kind of professionalism.'

'I'll go and get Mrs. Libnitz,' I said, though what help that would be I could not imagine.

As I went out of the room, Dr. Laver was saying, 'Nothing will induce me to send a report from this clinic which reeks of secular piety.'

He was totally absorbed in his argument to the exclusion of all else; I felt that if Douglas, or even he himself, had been dying, he would have pursued it to the last breath. I ran down the stairs. Mrs. Libnitz was in the hall talking to a burly man who had come to complain because Iris had parked her car in the entrance to a field so that he could not get his tractor past it.

'Oh please help us,' I said breathlessly. 'Something terrible has happened.'

We ran up the stairs. Iris was by this time standing on a chair; I could see that if she succeeded in getting the window open she would fall out. Dr. Laver was telling her that people are conditioned by the language they use. Douglas was hanging limply, arms dangling; whether he found this more comfortable, or had fainted, was not clear. The farm labourer put Iris to one side, then placed an enormous hand each side of the frame and heaved. The window shot up.

'Don't let go of it!' I shouted, afraid it would come down again and decapitate Douglas before we dragged him clear. We pulled him into the room and he sat on the floor in a crumpled heap, his face in his hands. 'Put your head between your legs,' Iris commanded brusquely.

'My head is bursting with blood as it is.'

Dr. Laver said, 'I think we've all had a tiring day, so we'll close shop now.' He walked out of the room.

Douglas said, 'I had a vision of some sort while I was hanging there. I'll just stay here and think about it for a while.'

Iris said, 'Everyone is mad today.' It was not a word much used in our clinic.

6

MY father had arranged for a memorial tablet to be
placed in the graveyard at the back of our church, and
Mother's ashes were to be scattered on the Saturday.
Eleanor came down for this occasion. We took her
inclusion as natural although she had not been a
frequent visitor in the days when Mother was alive.
Whether it was Eleanor's participation in our lives, I
don't know, but about this time, although I would never
have addressed him in this way, I found that I was
thinking of my father as Stewart. It was as though he
was moving out of my close family circle and becoming
a different person. Perhaps in some ways this freed him,
but it also made him subject to the hazards of a more
objective appraisal. For years I had, so to speak,
swallowed him whole without savouring the special taste
of him; now I was no longer so undiscerning.

The ceremony was short. I had expected to be upset
but wasn't. I could not associate the fine grey ashes with
Mother. Stewart was not upset either, and I think this
confused him. He was restless afterwards. We walked
round the graveyard reading the inscriptions on the
tombstones and he was very moved by the jam jars containing primroses and violets. On the east side of the
church there was a big, vigorous forsythia, its branches
clotted with yellow. He came to it unexpectedly and
caught his breath as though its vibrant display was too
much for him. Eleanor, who seemed to have resented
the church atmosphere, was making comments about
the church porch and the possible date of the chancel,

her tone emphasising that to her this was just another
ancient monument.

Beyond the low wall of the graveyard there was pasture-
land where cows grazed, a gentle, unemphatic country
landscape. Stewart leant his elbows on the wall and said,
'How peaceful it is!' We stood silent beside him. A breeze
parted the long grass. Somewhere, so far away it scarcely
disturbed the quiet, a motor bike zoomed along a country
lane. He said, 'She would like to lie here.' His voice was
choked.

A feeling, so fierce I had no idea what caused it,
swept over me. 'She would like to have been buried in
London,' I said.

He looked at me in amazement; his face was working
and seemed in imminent danger of falling apart. I
walked away to give us both time to recover. He was my
father and I loved him; he was going through a very dis-
tressing experience and he was trying to be brave about
it; now, more than at any other time, he needed my
support. But I could not give it and I was not even
sorry. I was angry. I did not know why I was angry, but
that made no difference; my whole body throbbed with
the pain of my anger so that I wanted to cry out loud. I
stared up at the forsythia, brilliant against the blue sky.
I loved my father and I loved my mother and I did not
like myself, but there was nothing I could do about it.

After a minute or two Eleanor joined me. 'Stewart has
gone to have a few words with the verger,' she said.

I did not answer. She plucked a sprig of rosemary and
rubbed it between her fingers.

'You're incredible!' I thought she meant to rebuke me,
but she went on, 'You are both quite incredible, talking
about where she would like to have been buried as
though it had any relevance. Those ashes . . . don't you
realise what they were?'

'I suppose so.' I looked at her in surprise.

'You suppose so!' Her face was pale. 'I shall give my body to science if anyone wants it by the time I'm through with it.' She sucked her breath in and shut her lips tightly.

'You could do with a cup of tea,' I said. 'I'll go home and put the kettle on.'

She gave me a lop-sided smile, knowing that I was glad of an excuse to escape.

Stewart seemed to have put my outburst out of his mind and over tea he talked about the graveyard and how nicely it was maintained, including me in the conversation as though he was sure that I agreed with every word that he spoke. After tea, he said he must see the vicar. I was going to a meeting of the local amateur dramatic society.

'We can't leave you alone,' he said to Eleanor.

'Why ever not?' She reacted with the irritation of a person who is used to organising her own life.

'I wouldn't dream of it.' He was going through a spell when he could not bear to be left alone and he had adopted the attitude that no one should be alone. It was a pleasant evening and I think Eleanor would have enjoyed an hour or so on her own.

'You can come to the vicarage with me,' he said.

She did not like his insistence but she controlled her impatience. Again, I was aware of her refashioning her personality.

'I'm not very good at making conversation with reverend gentlemen.' Her voice sounded amused: she was not going to make an issue of this.

'He's a very interesting man; quite an authority on Gilbert White.'

Eleanor said drily, 'That makes all the difference.'

He was impatient to leave. Since Mother's death he had been anxious to make more contacts in the village. He talked to people over the wall when he was gardening, he had made the acquaintance of a solicitor who lived further along the lane and had been to his house for lunch-time drinks, and he had visited the vicar several times.

At lunch the next day he told us he would like to call on Miss Maud. He said he was very moved that she had sent a wreath. Eleanor announced her intention of working in the garden, if he would trust her to weed the gravel path. She was firm about it. He asked me to accompany him, and as I was still feeling guilty about my behaviour in the graveyard I said that I would.

'I shall have to be back by five o'clock, though, because I'm going out,' I said as we left the house. 'But I don't suppose Miss Maud will expect us to stay long.'

'She might want us to stay for tea.'

'I don't think she lives in that style now.'

'There's nothing stylish about having tea, is there?' he asked irritably.

It was a fine, warm day and we took the footpath across the fields to Miss Maud's house.

'What are you doing this evening?' Stewart did not ask as a matter of casual concern, but as though he wanted to find out about my life to see where he fitted into it. He had made several enquiries of this kind recently.

'I'm going out for a drink with Bill Harrison.'

'I thought that was all finished.'

'We're not engaged, but we still see each other from time to time.'

'Isn't that rather unusual?'

'Not really. We like each other.'

'Do you . . .' He hesitated. 'I mean, are you . . . have you . . . ?'

'No.'

He looked puzzled. Like so many of his generation it had taken him a long time to accept the ideas of the young on premarital sex, but having once come to terms with the situation it seemed impossible for him to conceive of the young having friendship without sex. I could tell that he did not believe me.

'Why don't you want to marry him?' he asked.

'Just because.'

We walked in silence for a few hundred yards, then he said, 'How old are you now?'

'Thirty plus.'

'*Are* you?' He gave me an unbelieving look; although he did not want to lose me, he did not like to think that I was unconcerned about my unmarried state. After another hundred yards, he said, 'Don't you want to get married?'

'Not just like that.'

'It isn't possible to have a sensible conversation with you if you keep saying things like "just because" and "not just like that",' he said irritably.

'Never mind.'

'Of course I mind. I like to know what is going on in your life. You're my daughter.'

'It hasn't worried you until now,' I pointed out.

'There was always Mother before. I assumed she knew these things.'

I had not confided in my mother. There has to be something one keeps to oneself. Now I wondered if my mother would have minded about Reuben. Stewart would have been horrified, but I could not be sure what her reaction would have been. I was beginning to realise how much there was that I had not known about her. Bill Harrison had wanted to marry me and settle down and rear children who would go into his law firm and join the tennis club. Reuben was a gypsy. I suppose his life followed a pattern, too, but to me it did not seem to. He was attractive and did not have any plans for me beyond the immediate sexual act. Bill had found out about Reuben and he had been scandalised. He had

said there was talk about me in the village because I
went after the gypsies.

'They don't talk about me because I go out with you.'

'That's a foul thing to say.'

'Foul!' I still could not see what was foul about it. Bill
seemed to think I was rebelling against my parents but
that I was pushing it too far. But I was not rebelling
against anything. I accepted people as they came; I
liked Reuben and I had not thought when I slept with
him that I had stepped outside of anything. Perhaps I
belonged outside, whatever 'outside' meant.

Stewart was still pursuing his investigation. He asked,
'Didn't your mother talk to you about marriage?'

'Whatever you do, don't get married!' had been my
mother's advice. I had never been sure how seriously she
meant it. I said, 'I expect she knew that I'd do my own
thing.'

'There you go again! Why can't young people talk
intelligibly?'

'I'm sorry.' I put my arm through his. 'I know I'm
grumpy. I don't seem able to help myself.'

He squeezed my arm and said, 'I know, darling; I
know.'

We walked in silence for a few minutes and then I
said, 'I've been thinking about Scotland. It would be
rather fun, wouldn't it? I telephoned Dorothy the other
night and I could go to her for a week-end in the
autumn.'

'Scotland?'

'Ross and Cromarty.'

'What about Ross and Cromarty?'

'I thought perhaps you were upset because I hadn't
seemed keen to go.'

'I'd forgotten all about it. Do you want to go?'

'Not if you don't.'

'I don't think I want to go all that way just now.'

We could see Miss Maud's house at the edge of the field. I hoped she would be in and that we should not have to make this journey again.

'Why do you want to see Miss Maud?' I asked.

'I want to thank her for sending the wreath.'

But it was more than that. He had talked about her a lot lately. To him, she seemed to represent an authority and a stability which he had lost and wanted to retrieve. In the past, he had referred to her as a 'dotty old thing', but now he spoke of her as having belonged to a way of life that was good and had passed away. I had the fantastic idea that if she had received him in the style in which he imagined she lived, he would have been prepared to shut himself up here with her and ignore a world he liked less and less.

But however much one may shut away the world, there are some things with which one has to come to terms; and it was evident as we approached the house that Miss Maud had come to terms with the necessity of feeding herself. Old Mr. Leveridge had employed a gardener and an under-gardener, but both had gone now. Gone, too, were the rose garden, the flower beds and the herb garden. The rose garden had been put down to vegetables and ramshackle chicken coops had been erected where the herb garden had once flourished; the flower beds and the croquet lawn had been left to Nature, which had done its usual untidy job. Miss Maud was at this moment feeding the hens. A battered straw hat decorated with roses shaded her eyes and the rose motif was dimly repeated in the ankle-length gingham dress; a pair of Wellington boots completed the outfit.

Stewart, who was wearing a neat grey suit and an immaculate blue and white striped shirt, was taken aback; but Miss Maud greeted him with such aristocratic assurance that he was reconciled to her appearance. 'How delightful!' She tucked the grain bowl under one arm and shook hands with both of us. 'Now you must come and take tea with me.'

We walked past a flower bed where a rambler rose fought a grim battle with foxgloves and ground elder. 'I've had to let Chapman go,' she said. 'The garden was getting too much for him.'

'Chapman?' Stewart repeated.

'The head gardener.'

Stewart said, 'Ah yes.' Only yesterday he had commented on Chapman's tombstone as we walked round the graveyard. 'Died nineteen hundred and fifty nine, aged ninety-one years,' he had read out.

Miss Maud led us to the front door which stood open. She paused in the porch to take off her Wellington boots, revealing small feet and slim ankles encased in grey silk stockings. The porch was cluttered with croquet mallets, deck chairs, folding green-baize tables, and geraniums in pots. The great wall mirror which I remembered from my childhood visit was hanging in the hall; it was dusty and tarnished but still looked imposing by virtue of its size. Beneath it was a carved wooden chest piled with letters, seed catalogues, calendars and newspapers yellow with age. There were also a lot of bills and several rate demands. Miss Maud put her hand to the wall and a bell jangled in the rear of the house. 'We'll take tea in here,' she said. We went into the drawing-room. Even in this warm weather the room struck chill and there was a smell which, after a glance at the discoloured patches on the outside wall, I decided must be damp. In spite of the damp, the wallpaper with its faded pattern of fleur-de-lys was still elegant. The room had been hoping for us. The grand piano to one side of the window, the china cabinet on the long wall, demanded admiration; the chairs, couch and side tables, carefully positioned on the chinese carpet, were waiting to receive guests.

Miss Maud said, 'Please sit down. Bridget will bring tea.' She went out of the room.

Stewart said, 'Well!' He sat on the couch and a puff of dust rose in the air. I went to the piano and touched a key; no sound came but the imprint of my finger was left on the ivory. I rubbed at it guiltily. 'Was Bridget one of the maids?' I asked.

Stewart nodded.

'How long ago did she die?'

'Sometime in the nineteen-sixties, I believe.' He looked shocked. 'What a terrible thing! I had no idea.'

'I think she's quite happy.'

'But she's only in her early seventies. That's no age nowadays.'

'I wonder what Bridget is getting us for tea,' I said.

He looked dismayed and then smiled; I realised that it was a long time since he had smiled. He said, 'I don't suppose it will be dainty cucumber sandwiches.'

There was a family portrait on the wall; the mother sitting stiff-backed on the couch, the father standing erect behind her, three little girls strung out beside the mother and a boy looking cramped on a footstool. None of them looked very happy although one of the little girls had a gleam in her eyes which I thought I recognised.

'What happened to the brother and the sisters?' I asked.

'One of the girls died quite young; the other was still alive when we first came to live here. I believe the brother went abroad.'

A distant rumbling and a clatter of crockery told us that tea was on the way. Stewart got up and held open the door. There was a dusty patch on the seat of his trousers. Miss Maud came in wheeling a trolley. 'I think Bridget can go now,' she said briskly. She spoke as though we were all aware that Bridget was a convention which must be observed. Perhaps this was the only way in which Miss Maud could undertake the task of looking after the house and still remain its mistress.

She poured strong tea into fluted china cups. There was a chocolate loaf on a tarnished silver dish; with relief I identified it as the produce of the woman who kept the village post office. The scones probably came from the same excellent source. Stewart handed me cup and saucer and brought milk and sugar.

'I was talking to the vicar yesterday about March House,' he said to Miss Maud. 'He thinks that at one time it belonged to the Verney family, but I rather doubt that. I was sure that you would know.'

'What nonsense that man does talk! Of course it never belonged to the Verneys.' Miss Maud was delighted to talk about March House, mentioning many people of whom I had never heard as though they were still important features of the neighbourhood.

As I listened, I realised something I had never understood before. Miss Maud was as isolated as my mother had been. Unlike Mother, however, she belonged here: her trouble was that no one else did. The important families had melted away, their houses had been sold, and the village was full of people who had moved in over the years since the war. The structure of the society Miss Maud's parents had known had broken down and Miss Maud was now the only person who belonged. The problem set by finding oneself living in a world where no one else belonged must have been daunting. Custom and acceptance are vital; what happens when maintenance of the kind they provide is no longer available? By now, Miss Maud probably had only a vague memory of how things ought to be.

Stewart, who had responded with courtesy to Miss Maud's account of the history of March House, decided it was time to do some reminiscing of his own.

'I remember that just after we moved here the Percivals were at March House.' I was surprised to realise that he had known March House long before I went to work there. I had always thought of it as being a place where I had a life unknown to my parents, where they could not even visualise my existence. Stewart was saying, 'The Percivals had a garden party. That must have been . . . when . . . nineteen forty seven?' He turned to me. 'Before you were born, my dear.'

'Well, yes, it must have been.' I did so hope that he was not going to become sentimental: that he should know March House was bad enough, but that he should establish special claims to it was unbearable.

'My dear wife was a young woman then.' He looked out of the window, summoning up his ghosts. 'I can see her now . . .'

Miss Maud glanced at him sharply. 'I am going to cut this cake. I hope you will have some. It is delicious.'

Stewart, who had not interrupted her when she was telling him how her parents had attended balls at March House, continued firmly, 'You are one of the few people who can remember Lillian as she was then, so I know you will excuse me talking to you about her. She was very beautiful. When we went to that garden party people turned to stare at her.'

Miss Maud said quietly, 'Yes, I do remember how striking your wife was.' She raised the teapot and held out a hand for my cup.

'I couldn't believe that this beautiful girl had married me. If you say that kind of thing to young people nowadays they sneer.' His voice had become bitter and I felt that he was getting at me. 'There is no romance any more; the very idea embarrasses them. They don't mind taking drugs and sleeping around; it's only the idea of being in love that embarrasses this unshockable generation!'

When Miss Maud had filled my cup, she caught hold of my free hand and gave it a shake.

Stewart said deliberately, 'But I was in love, and I remained in love all my life, right to the very end.' His face was like marble.

I said, 'We came to thank you for sending the wreath, Miss Maud. It was very kind of you. We sent the flowers to the church and to the hospital afterwards; it seems such a waste to . . .'

Stewart said loudly, 'I can't believe that she's gone. Every time I go into the house. . . .' He choked over the words.

Miss Maud picked up the teapot and crossed the room to where he was sitting. 'You know, you will have to stop this,' she said in a matter-of-fact voice as she poured tea. 'I know it's very upsetting for you and I'm glad you came to talk to me. But you mustn't get into a habit of letting yourself go. It's bad for your daughter. And you mustn't lean on her, either, just because she's still at home with you, which is very unusual these days.'

I could not bear to see how he took this, I was so distressed for him. I turned in my chair and examined the china in the cabinet. I could hear the clink of his spoon as he stirred his tea. To my amazement, he said meekly, 'Yes, you are right, of course.' He sounded like a naughty child who has been waiting to be told how far it can go.

'Of course I'm right! Most young women have left home by the time they are twenty. The days have gone when daughters can be expected to sacrifice themselves for their fathers.'

'Yes,' he sighed sadly. 'We must let the young people lead their own lives.'

'*You* did, didn't you?'

'I'm not sure.' He examined the idea as though it had not occurred to him before. I turned to look at him.

'When I was a boy I wanted to be a farmer, but no one took me seriously.'

'You shouldn't have let that stop you.'

'It's hard to take yourself seriously if no one else does.'

'So you did something they were prepared to take seriously?'

'I went to Oxford.'

When he was with strangers he usually mentioned that he had been to Oxford, offering the information as he might have shown a passport. But today it was a gesture of defeat.

I had never heard him talk like this before, usually he spoke deferentially about his parents and his over-bearing sisters. I was aware of pain. The awareness was new, but the pain was not. It had always been there and probably explained the withdrawals which had baffled me as a child. Now I had a glimpse of him as a young man, painfully sensitive and unsure, accepting his family's assessment of himself and dutifully starting on a career which would cripple his spirit. Later, he had paid them back by marrying my mother.

'My father was a Victorian, too,' Miss Maud was say-ing as though this explained everything. 'When my mother died it was assumed that I would look after him and my sister. I was very attractive and a lot of men wanted to marry me, but I turned them away. My sister was an invalid and I knew that I couldn't leave her alone with him. There were times when I thought of killing him; but one doesn't do that sort of thing.'

Neither Stewart nor I knew quite how to take the remark. She sensed our uneasiness and said, 'Well, why not? It would have been very sensible. He didn't enjoy his life, but I should have enjoyed mine much more. I should have had this house and his money would have come to me at a time when I could have profited by it; I could have married, or if that didn't appeal to me, I could have had as many men as I wanted.'

'People in the village used to say how well you looked after your father, Miss Maud,' Stewart said, trying gently to restore normality to the conversation.

'The doctor told him he mustn't eat so much because it was bad for his heart. But he liked good food and I saw no reason why he shouldn't have it. I suppose you might say I fed him to death.' Stewart smiled, but I thought she meant exactly what she said. She picked up the silver dish. 'Another piece of this delicious cake?' It was a theatrical cliché and indicated how much she was enjoying herself. Stewart, resolutely determined to treat the matter as a joke, accepted a second piece of cake.

It was far from a joke. Miss Maud had grown up in this house with a brother and two sisters. I had longed for brothers and sisters and had been disappointed when my parents only provided dolls. But listening to Miss Maud, and looking at this room, I found no hint of remembered happiness. The secrets of this house were dark ones. Stewart was maintaining a conversation of precarious normality about flower borders, but I was afraid that this could not last. Miss Maud would not stay long with hollyhocks and lupins.

Somewhere at the rear of the house a door opened. Miss Maud half-turned her head to listen. Footsteps sounded in the corridor. I was unreasonably apprehensive. I have no idea whom I expected to see when the door opened, but it was not Dr. Laver. He came into the room cradling a large tabby cat in his arms. When he saw us he said, 'I came to buy eggs.'

Miss Maud introduced him to Stewart and they attempted to shake hands; the cat scratched Stewart. It was a deep scratch and bled profusely. Miss Maud hurried out of the room. Dr. Laver, still cradling the cat, said, 'No need to be disturbed; by the look of that blood you are not in the least anaemic.' He did not

91

acknowledge my presence and I was glad of that, although afterwards I thought it strange. He tickled the cat behind the ear and said what splendidly independent creatures cats were, not like dogs who were forever trying to ingratiate themselves with humans. The cat purred like a dynamo all the while gazing hostilely at Stewart. Miss Maud returned with a grey-looking roll of bandage. Stewart, who had been prepared to risk the chocolate cake, was having none of the bandage. Dr. Laver unhooked the cat from his jacket and, saying something about cold water, led Stewart away.

'There's blood on your carpet,' I said to Miss Maud. 'Shall I sponge it? The stain won't come out once it dries.'

I went into the corridor. Dr. Laver must have taken Stewart to the downstairs lavatory; I could hear him saying, 'Not what I call full-bodied, mind you, but a good colour nevertheless.' He fitted into the house much better than Stewart. If I had never met him before I would not have been surprised if Miss Maud had introduced him as a distant relative or even the brother who had gone abroad. I made my way to the kitchen where I found a grimy cloth in the sink and wetted it under the tap. When I returned to the drawing-room the cat was sitting on the trolley licking the top of the chocolate cake while Miss Maud caressed its head. 'His name is Pewter,' she said. She watched me for a moment or two and then said crossly, 'Do you usually insist on doing the cleaning when you come to tea?'

I reflected on this for a moment and then replied, 'I thought perhaps the sight of blood might upset Bridget.'

There was a prolonged scuffle and a lot of squawking in the corridor and Dr. Laver came in carrying a scrawny hen, followed by Stewart looking pale with his handkerchief tied round his hand and feathers on his coat sleeve. The cat and the hen were obviously old enemies and while Dr. Laver and Miss Maud contrived to keep them apart, we made our farewells and departed.

'What an extraordinary man!' Stewart said as soon as we were out of the front door. I did not comment on this because Dr. Laver had not seemed as extraordinary in that house as he had done at the clinic. 'Wherever did he come from? I've never seen him before, and he's hardly the sort of person one would overlook.'

There was no sign of a car and the country buses did not run on Sunday afternoon.

Stewart said, 'He's no more a doctor than I am! What doctor would wear a suit and a shirt like that? Do you think we should tell the police?'

'He only came for eggs.'

We walked the length of the field in silence, throwing long shadows across the grass. I knew that I should explain to Stewart about Dr. Laver but I could not bring myself to do it. My parents had been to March House in the past and now my father had encountered Dr. Laver. I wanted the unreal world of the clinic and the real world of my home to remain in their separate compartments. Beyond the field, the footpath turned sharply to the right and traversed a field of oats. Mill House slipped out of sight.

7

IRIS, Douglas and Di were having an informal meeting in my room. Earlier in the week they had decided to reject hypnotism and now they were trying to marshall the arguments they would shortly present to Dr. Laver.

'I don't have to be hypnotised,' Di said. 'I know what he's going to say about me without that.'

'*You* are going to be the one who says it.' Iris assumed the role of Devil's Advocate automatically; then, recovering herself, added, 'Or so I understand it.'

'I'll say what he's fed into me,' Di rephrased obligingly.

'It won't be fed into you, Di. Something which is already within you will be revealed.' Iris was standing by the mantelshelf staring in the mirror, whether at herself or at Di it was hard to tell.

Di said, 'I'm not revealing anything to him. He's kinky, with those cut-glass eyes.'

'In what way do you mean "kinky"?' Iris turned her head slightly, definitely looking at Di now. Douglas looked at her, too. He had become very prickly since his liaison with Eddie.

Di brooded. I could understand her problem. Since she had worked at the clinic so many things she had thought to be kinky had been judged acceptable that she was finding it hard to come up with something that Iris and Douglas would find impressive. 'I've known lots of fellows,' she said, unwittingly playing her strongest card. 'And this one's kinky.'

Iris looked gravely in the mirror. After a moment, she raised her hands and folded them over her head so that the cloud of white hair was almost eliminated.

Di said, 'Anyway, anything I revealed would be pretty crude.'

Douglas said, 'The subconscious *is* crude.'

'But this isn't the subconscious.' Iris tilted her head, glancing at the mirror image at that angle where one has the illusion of catching it unawares. 'It is a rediscovery of one's past self.'

'I've spent the last year trying to get away from my past,' Douglas retorted. 'He can hypnotise the clients if he wants to, but he's not going to hypnotise me.'

'How could we justify that?' Iris asked the mirror. 'Our clients are encouraged to examine things in themselves which they will find disturbing, so shouldn't we be prepared to do the same?'

'More and more I am coming to subscribe to the "tea and sympathy" school of therapy.'

'Why worry about the clients?' Di asked. 'The poor sods never get to see the psychiatrist.'

Iris smiled and the woman in the mirror smiled back. Douglas said, 'Now that Dr. Laver is here it will be different.'

'He hasn't seen many clients so far, has he? If you ask me, he's more interested in us than the clients.'

Iris looked dubiously at the woman in the mirror. Something, some trick of light and shade, had disturbed her; or perhaps it was that she had looked so long that the image had ceased to seem familiar, just as one can sometimes be struck by the strangeness of a familiar word.

'What do you think about all this, Ruth?' Di asked.

'I agree with the tea and sympathy idea. In fact, I plan to leave here and run a teashop.' The disquiet which I sensed in Iris was affecting me.

'You mean you would get more of a kick running a teashop than working here?' Douglas seemed glad to welcome distraction.

'I'd make my own bread and lots of different jams. And I'd make muffins, too; everyone talks of muffins as though they'd gone out with the Great Auk, but why shouldn't we have muffins again in England?'

'Why not, indeed,' Douglas murmured. 'Will you perform this service to the nation on your own, or will you bring back holy matrimony along with muffins?'

'My husband will run the local pub; not the big one with ivy growing over the stone walls and the cobbled carriageway and horse brasses and genuine thirteenth century wood beams; the one at the unfashionable end of the high street with a piano in the back room and lino-leum on the floor and a picture of the local fire brigade on their 1911 engine.'

'Very dull,' Douglas said.

'Stimulating, articulate people will be regarded with suspicion and at the first whiff of culture they will be asked to leave.'

Iris said, 'Once, a long time ago, I wanted to be a missionary.'

There was a startled silence, then Di said, 'What would you have used for God?'

Iris turned away from the mirror. 'It was a long time ago.' She seemed as startled by the revelation as we were.

I was glad when Dr. Laver buzzed on the intercom. and asked me to come into his room.

He was sitting at his desk going through the register. He had been doing this for several weeks now, but little seemed to have come of it. He was still wearing the same suit and shirt and I began to wonder whether he was inextricably built into them and unable to step free.

'I have been studying the register and the case histories,' he said.

This seemed too self-evident to warrant a reply.

'Who is responsible for accepting the clients?' he asked.

'Iris.'

He made a face and I said, 'The clinic would have closed if it hadn't been for Iris. She has kept it going by sheer strength of will.'

'You think well of Iris?'

'I think she is very able.'

'Rather lukewarm praise.'

'She has a lot of courage and she is very ambitious, not just for herself, but for women generally. In another age she would have been a suffragette and enjoyed going to prison. In a way, she's missed her period.'

'What nonsense you do talk!' He looked sour. I had noted before that praise of other people, however lukewarm, did not please him. 'In an earlier age, Iris would have been mother of a large family of boys and her only rebellion would have been keeping a diary. Very few people break out of the patterns of the past. You, for example, would be looking after your sick mother and then your sick father and then you'd find another sick relative to look after.'

'I don't see myself as a downtrodden female.'

'How do you see yourself? A loner, perhaps?'

'No. That's just as bad.'

'Then what?'

'I'm me. And before you laugh — what about the way you talked to Iris about the language in her reports? I don't like *your* language. You always talk about people as specimens, loner, isolate, middle class. I don't see myself that way.'

'How would you describe yourself?'

'Someone who likes to find her own way . . . '

'Inexact as well as being a delusion.'

'Because it's inexact it allows for complexity and contradiction, growth and change. But "loner" is something that types a person for ever; they spend the rest of their life living up to it — like "rebel".'

'The delusion is what principally worries me. It is

impossible for anyone to find their own way. We are all born into a way of life—even you, Ruth, had a mother and father, a family group; you went to school and began to see yourself as part of a larger group. Or, at least, that is what should have happened. But it seems to me that even for an only child you are very resistant to seeing beyond the family group.'

I wanted to strike back, to tell him that when I came into the room I had thought he was the prisoner of his suit and shirt. But I was inhibited by the memory of our meeting at Miss Maud's to which he had never referred. He had seen me with my father. I did not want the two worlds to mingle. So I tried to be conciliatory.

'I expect you are right,' I said, and then made one of those Freudian errors. 'It's just that none of this psychological, sociological talk seems real to me.'

He homed in on target. 'What do you mean by this distinction between the real and the unreal? Do you, for example, subscribe to the silly notion that a collier's life is more real than an Oxford don's? All people's lives are real or unreal, take your choice which, but they're all the same. And the things which happen to people are either real or unreal, even their dreams.'

'Bugger their dreams!'

'Now, there's a nice bit of the real coming out in you.'

The door opened and Douglas came in. 'Are you ready for us?' he asked. Iris was standing thrustfully behind him. They came in without waiting for an answer. Di was the last; she had the look she often had at case conferences, as though her desirable body was an embarrassment and she was not sure what to do with it. I was comforted by this, because it was familiar; Di had not changed, but I was not sure of the other two.

After they had seated themselves there was silence. This was a technique which both Iris and Douglas had employed successfully in the past. It did not work in this case. Silence was a vacuum which Dr. Laver filled. As those bright eyes looked at each one of them in turn I had again the feeling that he knew things about people which were hidden, not only from others, but from themselves. He said, 'There is a lot of tension in this room. What are we to do about it?'

Di said helpfully, 'We could open the window.'

I hoped they might leave it at that; but Iris said, 'I suppose anxiety is our particular occupational hazard. Are you saying that the level is unacceptably high?'

'I find the level of stress extremely high. In fact, I find the situation here quite unacceptable.'

'I hope we are going to be able to discuss this quietly and rationally,' Iris said. 'A certain amount of stress is to be expected, is it not? We are, after all, probably more self-aware than most people. Perhaps that is another occupational hazard, but surely you would agree that it can also be a positive factor?'

Dr. Laver had until this moment been responding to Iris in a provocative and lively manner. Now the current of energy was switched off. He seemed no longer interested in us and it had the effect of making one feel suddenly cold. He spoke looking down at the surface of the desk. 'Constant self-analysis renders a person incapable of taking a clear view of anyone, particularly himself. It is a distorting glass in which we see a creature so fragmented as to be barely recognisable as a human being.' This statement was made with sombre conviction.

Iris turned her head away; the movement was sharp and caught my eye. I noticed the tension of jaw and throat and wondered if she had been pushing herself too far lately. Then I forgot about Iris because I became aware that the room was rather small and I wanted to get out of it. I looked at my watch; it was a quarter past ten. In half an hour I could suggest that I should make coffee. Half an hour was a long time.

Dr. Laver studied us all; at first, we seemed to perplex him and he narrowed his eyes, bringing us into focus. Energy began to flow from him again, but when he spoke his voice had a quality I had not heard before, between pleading and tenderness. 'I should like to ask for your trust. Self-analysis is harmful and ultimately destructive. There are surer, and gentler, ways of allowing the hidden self to speak. When we analyse ourselves we do it with our conscious mind; but our conscious mind is the jailor of that hidden self.' Iris was looking at him with the same fascination with which she had examined the woman in the mirror. Now, looking back, I believe that he had already begun to hypnotise her. He repeated, 'Our conscious mind is a jailor. Do we really believe in the tyrant who sets the prisoner free?'

Douglas spoke for the first time. His voice sounded level and reasonable as it did when he was angry. 'Another way of looking at it is that over many years we learn to effect a balance between the positive and destructive sides of our nature and it would be wilful to destroy that balance. I speak as a layman in these matters, of course.'

'And who decides which is the destructive side?'

Douglas's face became blank.

'But you may be right, of course,' Dr. Laver conceded silkily. 'It would be nothing short of monstrous to interfere with that rare person who has effected such a balance at not too great a cost.'

Di, who was sitting near to me, whispered, 'Christ! It doesn't do to step out of line with him.'

Dr. Laver turned sharply to look at her and she hunched her shoulders and folded her arms beneath her breasts. She would never have a confrontation with him; I had the feeling that of the people in this room she was the least likely to fall under his spell. Perhaps he sensed this; he turned towards Iris who had been unusually quiet. 'I think that this is the time when we should make the experiment to which we agreed previously.'

It was an outrageous statement; there had been no such agreement and I waited for one of them to tell him so. But they said nothing. It was as though he had laid down his terms for peace and they felt constrained to accept them. Or was it as simple as that? Was Iris curious about the woman in the mirror, just as I had been curious about the dark secrets of Miss Maud's house, in spite of my fear?

Iris said, 'What do I have to do?'

Douglas turned to her in consternation.

Dr. Laver said, 'How are you most comfortable?' Iris clasped her hands in her lap and frowned down, willing them to be quiet. Dr. Laver said, 'Never mind about your hands; relax your shoulders.'

Douglas put out a hand and Dr. Laver said, 'Yes, touch her by all means; it may help her,' and Douglas withdrew his hand as though it had been stung.

Dr. Laver said, 'You are tired and tense. You probably have a slight headache. I will take that away when you go to sleep.' He spoke in a light, conversational tone so that we supposed he had not yet begun the business of hypnotism. I waited, expecting that he would give the same impression of complete absorption in the subject which Iris and Douglas gave when they were talking to their clients.

He went on in the same light, easy voice, 'Try to think of something that is pleasing to you, something visual; water, perhaps? Do you like the sea?' Iris nodded. 'Good. Then lie back and float, let it carry you, gently, gently . . . It's a warm day and there is blue sky above you. The water is bearing you, taking all the weight.' He rambled on. I would have doubted if he had ever succeeded in hypnotising anyone had I not found myself feeling rather sleepy. I looked at Iris. Her head had rolled to one side, her eyes were closed, and her mouth was half-open, the

101

lips parted in a loose-jawed smile. She was asleep and looked peaceful in a bovine way.

I glanced at Douglas and Di. They both looked incredulous. Dr. Laver said, 'She *is* asleep. If you like I will send her into deep sleep and we can have a little demonstration. Has anyone got a needle?'

I said that I had one. I was glad to get out of the room. Perhaps I could ask Mrs. Libnitz to deliver the needle. But I found that something stronger than curiosity impelled me to return. When I re-entered the room Iris had not moved; she was no longer smiling and she was breathing differently. Dr. Laver took the needle and plunged it in her arm, just above the wrist; Douglas, Di and I all flinched, but Iris did not. He put the needle down on the blotter. There was a bubble of blood on Iris's arm and he dabbed at it with a piece of cotton wool. I felt sweat on my forehead.

Dr. Laver looked out of the window, one arm swung over the back of his chair, tapping the wooden frame. Tap, tap, tap . . . I was closer to him than the others and could see that he was trying to compose himself. When he turned and placed his hands on the table, his face was grave, but I had had a glimpse of his triumph. 'Now, we are going to find the reason for some of this tension.' He spoke in that same easy, quiet voice which for some inexplicable reason gave me a picture of snow flakes coming gently down, down, downy . . . I jerked upright. Dr. Laver was saying, 'You are coming out of deep sleep. You can hear my voice, can't you?' Iris nodded her head. 'I am going to send you back to your eighth birthday. It is the afternoon of your eighth birthday.'

There was silence. Gradually the silence was filled by sound. Many fields away a dog was barking excitedly. Further away still, only a faint trace on the air, church bells rang. Then, something nearer, at first a little alarming because it was unidentifiable: bath water

102

running away. Eddie! Strange that he was actually in this building, towelling himself, perhaps looking forward to toast and marmalade. A louder, more insistent noise: the buzzer on the switchboard downstairs. It seemed to buzz for a long time, perhaps Mrs. Libnitz was in the lavatory? Iris was breathing shallowly. Di scuffed her sandals on the floor. There was a scratching in the eaves where the martins were nesting and grit spattered the window pane.

Iris said, 'I can see the branches of an apple tree.'

Another silence. We were all breathing shallowly. Eddie flushed the lavatory. Mrs. Libnitz came up the stairs; we heard her open several doors, then she went past our door, saying just loud enough to be heard, 'If people aren't taking calls I wish they would tell me!'

Iris said, 'Close. Close about me. Branches.'

Dr. Laver said, 'Where are you?'

'I'm in the tree.' The voice was her adult voice, but the way in which she volunteered the information was child-like.

'What can you see from the tree?'

'People.'

I began to think that if Iris was going to be led at this pace through the events of her eighth birthday the most we need fear was boredom. Perhaps Douglas felt the same, because he took a deep breath and settled more comfortably in his chair.

'People,' Iris repeated with childish interest. 'My father is down there and my brothers.' There was a pause while presumably she inspected them and they her; then, 'Not all my brothers. Timmy isn't there.' This seemed to please her. 'Timmy is indoors crying. I can hear him crying through the open window.' She was speaking faster. 'They are all looking up at me, telling me to come down. I throw apples at them and hit Harry. I hate Harry. I hate Harry and Fergus and Hugh; and most of all I hate Timmy. I pushed Timmy in the fish pond. That's why

103

I'm up the tree.' She sat with a little smile on her face savouring this rediscovered triumph.

Dr. Laver was not prepared for her to rest on her laurels and he asked how she got down from the tree.

Iris began to talk about her father fetching a ladder. While her father was mounting the ladder I began to feel drowsy. I was aware of the people in the room, of Iris talking and Dr. Laver prompting her from time to time; then I seemed to hear a voice in my own head. There was something odd about the room, someone there, someone who should not have been there . . . I jerked myself awake. The action had moved on, leaving me behind. I did not know whether Iris was up the tree still or not. No one was speaking. Perhaps it was all over and Iris was coming round.

Dr. Laver said, 'What happened to make you push Timmy in the pond?'

Iris frowned. She appeared to have some difficulty with this. The corners of her mouth turned down. 'My birthday book,' she said in a grieving tone. 'My mother is reading my birthday book to me and Timmy. Timmy doesn't understand, but I do. He keeps interrupting and asking what is happening and what words mean. I answer him to show Mummy how much I understand. But she is looking at Timmy all the time.' Iris was grizzling. 'Timmy says "don't want any more of silly old book." I say to Mummy that I would like to hear some more, but she closes the book. Timmy runs into the garden. I run after him, very quietly across the grass. He is standing by the fish pond. I give a big push in the middle of the elastic that holds up his shorts.'

Iris sat quietly having delivered herself of this.

Di said, 'Kids do that sort of thing all the time.'

Douglas said, 'Mine certainly did.' He sounded fond and relieved.

Iris said, 'I . . . hate . . . all . . . little . . . boys.'

Dr. Laver drew the palms of his hands along the rim of the desk and then gave the wood a congratulatory pat. He said, 'I'm going to put you to sleep now, Iris.' The room was getting very hot. I began to feel sleepy again. Dr. Laver was saying, 'I am going to put you into deep sleep now, Iris. When you wake you will feel refreshed.'

'I doubt that any of us will,' Douglas said glumly.

But Iris did look very peaceful. As I watched her, I felt overpoweringly sleepy and I must have dozed off because I don't remember what happened when Iris finally woke. Then, a long way away, I heard Dr. Laver telling Douglas to think of something visual which he found pleasing and peaceful. I thought, 'Douglas can't have . . . surely, he can't . . .'

It was while Douglas was going to sleep that I saw the child sitting in the corner of the room; she was about three, I suppose, sitting on a low stool with a doll held tight in her arms. There were other voices in the room now, not Dr. Laver's or Douglas's.

She was holding the doll tight against her chest and she was thinking, 'Why don't they notice me? Please let them notice me; please let them notice me.' The feeling was so intense you would think it must break such a tiny thing. There was a lot of crossness in the room, the walls shook with it, they were going to keel over and come down . . . The little girl said in a high, tearful voice, 'Dolly's upset; Dolly's very, very upset.'

A woman came and knelt beside her. 'Poor Dolly!' She bent her golden head, smothering her face in the doll's. Over the golden head the child looked up at the man who stood hesitant in the centre of the room. 'Dolly's upset. Make Dolly better.'

He said, 'Would Dolly like to go for a walk, do you think?'

The woman said, 'Dolly wants to go to sleep.'

The child looked from one to the other. Sometimes

105

they played a game with a thimble; they clenched their hands and she had to guess which of them had the thimble. Now there wasn't any thimble, but she still had to choose. She began to cry because she couldn't play the game without the thimble. The woman put her arms round her and held her tight. She said, 'Oh, my baby, my baby!' Now, she was crying, too.

The man said, 'You're upsetting the child. I'll take her down to the corner shop to get a cow for her farmyard.'

The woman said, 'Little girls aren't interested in farm-yards.' She held the child away from her so that she could look into the little face. 'Do you want to go down to the corner shop to get a cow for your farmyard?'

The child picked up the doll which had fallen on to the floor. 'I'll ask Dolly.'

'Oh, you and Dolly! Go on then, go down to the corner shop and get your old cow.'

The man took the child's hand. 'It's all right, my pet. Mummy's not very well; she doesn't mean it.' He led the child away from the woman who was standing with her back to the room, looking out of the window and cry-ing.

The child had gone now; and where she had been was a side-table with a stack of files on it and a tupperware box containing Dr. Laver's lunch. My head was throb-bing and my ribs ached. I scarcely dared to look at the other people in the room for fear of what I might see written on their faces. Then I realised that after I had fetched the needle I had not returned to the chair in which I had been sitting previously; instead I had de-tached myself from the group and taken a chair near the window. I was slightly behind Dr. Laver and facing Douglas and Iris. Di was to my right; I could see her face in profile, but she would have had to turn round to see mine. However I had reacted to these unhappy ghosts, it seemed likely that no one had observed me. Iris was occupied with her own thoughts. Douglas was saying, 'Talking of refreshment, I propose to have coffee now. I don't know about anyone else.'

I said, 'I'll put the kettle on.' My voice sounded hoarse, but no one seemed to notice. It was a small thing, I suppose, after all that had happened. I got up and pointed myself in the direction of the door; as I walked I felt I was keeling over and it took an effort of will not to grasp at chairs for support. I went to the lavatory and dashed cold water on my face. After a minute or two I began to feel better. Dr. Laver must have stronger powers than he realised, and he had inadvertently connected me with some past happening in this house; I would take care not to attend his sessions in future. I went back to my room, made the coffee, and carried the tray into Dr. Laver's room.

Dr. Laver was talking about people who resist hypnosis; apparently they were invariably emotionally crippled and intellectually enchained. Dr. Laver said he was sorry for such people in a tone which suggested that he thought they deserved to be mutilated as well as crippled and enchained. It seemed that his session with Douglas had not been very satisfactory.

Di said to Dr. Laver, 'I promised to 'phone the leader of the play group about my kids, if you don't mind.' He looked surprised but shrugged his shoulders acquiescently. She took a cup of coffee and went out of the room.

Iris took a spoonful of sugar and spilt some of it in the tray. 'We all have a lot of thinking to do, and we need a period of quiet.'

Dr. Laver said, 'What kids was she talking about?'

'Her own,' Douglas answered. 'She has two, a boy and a girl.'

'By different men, I suppose?' Primly.

'By her husband.'

107

Iris said, 'A time for reflection; then we may be able to talk about it . . .'

'This Alec she is always 'phoning is her husband?'

'No, he's the man she lives with.'

Iris said loudly, 'The important thing is to be constructive about this.'

'Yes, yes, yes.' Dr. Laver was testy. He heaped sugar into his coffee and stirred vigorously. Then he took a packet of biscuits out of his drawer and swore because he could not get the cellophane wrapper off. He rummaged for scissors. There was some urgency about this; one might have thought him diabetic were it not for the sugar. When he had extracted a wheatmeal biscuit he looked up and seemed surprised to find us still there. 'I think we have concluded our experiments for this morning,' he said.

'What about Ruth?' Iris asked.

'Ruth is very obstinate. That is her defence.'

Douglas said, 'She is very sensible. Life is no place for the undefended.'

Dr. Laver took another wheatmeal biscuit and dipped it in his coffee.

When I returned to my room Di was there, reading a magazine. I began to open the morning's post. 'Dr Laver must have hypnotised me to some extent,' I said, 'because I found my mind wandering on to things quite unconnected with the clinic. I lost the thread of Douglas's recital.'

'There wasn't one. He went off and nothing happened except a lot of heavy breathing.'

'Didn't he say anything?'

'Not a thing. Dr. Laver kept telling him he was blocking something and how bad it was for him; but he just stayed blocked. I thought "Good on you, chum!"; but he didn't look as good as Iris when he came round.'

'How did he look?'

'As if he'd done himself a mischief.' She tossed the magazine down on the table. 'If you ask me, Dr. Laver's a warlock.'

'I don't know why Iris and Douglas allowed themselves to get involved in this silliness,' I said.

All that afternoon, the child cried in me.

In the evening, instead of going home, I cycled into Weston Market and went to the library. I told the assistant that I was interested in histories of the area, particularly in the old houses, such as March House. She fetched three books from the reserve stock and I settled down with them in the reference room. Two of the books contained a lot of information about farming methods and urban development, but were short on ghosts. I put them aside after a brief examination. This left me with 'Now fades the glimmering landscape' which purported to chronicle 'the life and times of a byegone era'. When I handed it to the assistant to be stamped, she said, 'No one has had this out for years. I expect you could keep it if you asked.'

Stewart said he was going to watch cricket on the village green. He took Punter with him. 'You'll have to mind he doesn't chase the ball,' I said as they departed. As soon as I had finished the washing-up I settled down with the book. There were a lot of illustrations and I looked at them first; there had been something familiar about the child and I was sure I had seen a portrait of her somewhere. But 'Now fades the glimmering landscape', while offering numerous rustics standing outside their cottage doors, had no pictures of solitary children. Nor were there any ghosts of interest. I read until it began to grow dark and Stewart returned.

I was glad to go to bed. But sleep would not come. The house grew quiet. I lay awake and was afraid. Then, because I feared sleep, it began to overwhelm me. But I am sure that I was not asleep when the child returned; I was in that area of half-waking, half-sleeping when thoughts slide past our guard. She was squatting up in bed, her feet beneath her, the toes cold against her buttocks. Voices came up the stairs.

'You shouldn't let yourself go like that in front of the child.'

'You don't know what it is to have a child! A bedtime story is all she has from you. I have her all day. I take her for walks, and play with her, and listen to her talking to Dolly. She talks and talks and talks to that doll; it never stops!'

'But this is what all mothers have to do, surely?'

'What is "a mother"? I don't know what it is, it's not *me*. I've got a little girl; I adore being with her. I do, I do! You don't believe that, do you? You think I don't love her because I want to get away from her sometimes. You're away from her all day.'

'I don't want to be away. I often think of you both during the day and wish I was here with you. I look forward to coming home; it distresses me so much that . . .'

'I look forward to you coming home so that we can go out together.'

'We can't leave the child.'

'Mrs. Mason would come.'

'I should have to fetch her, and take her back.'

'And that would be too tiring, wouldn't it? So what will you do? You'll work in the garden until it's dark, two hours, three hours out there; *that* won't be too tiring for you, because it's what you want to do.' The voice was rising to a high plateau. 'Well, *I* want to get out of this house. I must get out of this house, I must, I must . . .'

A door banged and the shuddering repercussions seemed to fill the house. In the dark bedroom, the child bent over the doll. There was a slit in its belly and her fingers tore at it and twisted inside, methodically pulling out the stuffing.

110

I was sitting trembling on the edge of the bed. There was a wrenching pain in my side. Perhaps I had appendicitis? I rather hoped so; it was an explanation I could live with. But before deciding in its favour, there was something I had to do. I pulled on my dressing-gown and went on to the landing. Punter was there. He raised his head, but was too sleepy to do more than wave his tail languidly. The moon was bright and I could see my way without needing any other light. I went down the stairs. In the hall there was an old oak chest. I had polished it last week; while I was polishing it I had thought that I must turn out the contents, which were of a sentimental nature. I removed the vase of flowers and raised the lid of the chest. The family album was large and I found it without difficulty. I went into the sitting-room and turned on the reading-lamp. It didn't take me long to find her. She was sitting on a chair and clutching the doll in her arms; my mother had written under the photo-graph, 'Ruth with Dollie.'

It should have been perfectly obvious, of course, from the first moment that I saw the child; but I had not been prepared to accept that the unreal world of the clinic and the real world of home were now in dangerous collabora-tion.

8

THE next day at breakfast I said that I was not going into the office; I felt I needed a rest. My father was pleased because he had been saying this for some time. I looked at him. He was my father again; my objectivity had not lasted long. Yet there had been a change. I could not regard him as Stewart, a person from whom I had detached myself; but neither could I return him to a time when he was a figure to be taken for granted, accepted as one of the unalterable facts of my life.

'Do you the world of good,' he said. 'Take a chair out into the garden.'

When you have a shock you should pick yourself up and get straight back into the swing of life before the effects have time to creep up on you. Give an inch, and it becomes increasingly difficult to keep your hold on normality. I searched my mind for other pieces of advice. Self-indulgence is a recipe for disaster. Yes, that was a good one. I took more toast and buttered it. Whatever else happens you have to keep going; one foot before the other, don't mind where you're going so long as you keep going. I assembled these bits and pieces of counsel meticulously, anxious not to leave anything out. I had no intention of doing anything about them, but I found pleasure in making as large a collection as possible to be flouted.

'I might stay away for the rest of the week,' I said.

'Why not? Today is Wednesday; no point in going back on a Thursday.'

Wednesday, Thursday, Friday all to myself. Whatever

would it be like?

'You could take Punter for a walk, only don't go wind-ward of the Hamiltons' or you'll have the most awful trouble with him . . .' He began to map out my day for me.

There was something wrong with me. If he looked at me closely he would see that I was hideously out of focus. But he had no need to look at me closely. I was his daughter, day by day and year by year he had created me, adding a line here, a shadow there, until I was safely matured. A rearrangement of the furniture in the sitting-room would have affected him deeply, but he did not look for, or expect, change in people. My mother had been more difficult to get on with because she noticed people: I hadn't realised that before.

'. . . have to learn to control your baser instincts!'

I looked at him, startled, but he was talking to Punter.

When he had gone I went back to bed. It was a warm, sunny day; I could hear the birds singing in the trees. The light breeze smelt of flowers and hay. It was the kind of day when it is sinful to be indoors, let alone in bed. I lay without moving.

Downstairs the french windows were open. There had been a fire at the school overnight and we had all been sent home. I propped my bike against the shed and walked round the side of the house and in through the open french windows. My mother was in the hall, speaking on the telephone. She was saying, 'Oh Sid, I *have* thought about it. But what's the use? You wouldn't leave the farm and I couldn't leave Ruth.' I turned and went out again quickly.

Once or twice when I was returning from the games field which was several miles from the school building I had seen her talking to the man who farmed the land beyond Mill House. There had been something un-familiar about them which had made an impression on me. Probably she was on her way home and he had been inspecting the crop; but they hadn't the look of people who have momentarily paused to greet each other. You would be surprised if next time you looked they weren't there; they belonged in the way that people in a painting belong to the scene along with the trees and the corn. I had never seen my mother look as if she belonged with a person before.

I got on my bike and rode away. I was full of fear for my father. Later in the month I was going away to guide camp; but I knew that now I must not go. I must be here because my mother was always happier when I was here and if I went away she might leave my father.

I looked at the curtains moving gently in the breeze and remembered how I had ridden back to the house the second time. There was nothing spontaneous about that arrival, and there had not been much that was spontaneous after that. I had perceived that my role was to stop my parents from harming each other.

But none of this was new to me, I had not blocked it; it didn't take psychoanalysis or hypnosis to bring it to the surface of my mind. What *was* new was that child holding the doll against the pain in her chest. I had always taken things in my stride, turned an amused gaze on life. The pain was new and I was afraid of it. The child had grown older and the pain had grown more intense. She had lain here in this bed and listened for the noises, the slamming of a door, the smashing of china on the stone-flagged kitchen floor; she had gone to sleep saying, 'Please God, don't let them quarrel, please, please don't let them quarrel tonight.' I told myself that I did not know this child, that she was a stranger who had invaded my mind. I was a quiet, sensible, practical, well-adjusted person; I had been told this many times by many people; the word 'serene' had even been mentioned. But whatever my mind tried to tell me, my body gave the lie to it. My body ached with the strain of holding fear at bay, ached with the strain of being torn two ways by people I loved.

When I was twelve I had had a lot of stomach trouble. My mother had taken me to the doctor who had diagnosed indigestion. Subsequently it was accepted that I could not eat rich food.

'Oh Mummy, Mummy, I feel so bad inside!'

'That must be the pork yesterday. Never mind, darling, we'll have fish today.'

I hadn't eaten pork since. The smell of it was sufficient to make my stomach muscles tighten with fear. It was when I was twelve that I found out about my mother and the farmer.

My mother and the farmer . . . How important had it been to my mother? I wondered. A little bit of excitement, something to break the monotony of her life? I would never know. Until this moment I had not wanted to know. Their love, if love it was, had been a thing of terror which threatened the structure of our lives. It had never occurred to me that we could have survived a crisis. As far as my father was concerned, I think I was right; people talk easily nowadays about infidelity and the breakdown of marriages, but he would not have been able to take it, it would have destroyed him. Or would it have done? Are our parents as fragile as we imagine? I only knew my parents in so far as their lives impinged on mine. Only this morning I had noted how little my father knew me. But was I any better? I had seldom thought of my parents as people who had a separate existence before I came into the world; nor had I imagined that anything of great moment happened to them in the times when we were not together. At least, not until the day that I heard my mother talking to the farmer.

I could hear other voices now, the room was full of them.

'Ruth is very self-sufficient . . .'

'Ruth doesn't want to go away to university; she loves her home too much . . .'

'. . . so sweet-natured, most of the young are so aggressive . . .'

'It's a tough world, she'd never find her way in it . . .'

'Ruth doesn't want to have a place of her own; she loves her home too much . . .'

'A rather unexpected sense of humour; there isn't much she misses . . .'

'Ruth is very self-sufficient; I sometimes wonder if she will ever get married . . .'

'She loves her home too much.'

I was cycling home through the country lanes. It was late and I was afraid they would be worried about me. My chest was tight and I couldn't pedal fast enough. At the next bend I would see the house. I was saying to my-self, 'Oh God, let it be all right; let the lights be on; don't let anything have happened to them.'

Perhaps I *was* always a little anxious coming back to the house. I was prepared to admit that: a little anxious. But saying to myself, 'Oh God, let it be all right; let the lights be on . . .' No, I really did not remember that!

I was always so self-contained. My mother said that I was self-contained. When I returned from parties she would come and sit on the edge of my bed and ask questions, enjoying youthful pleasures vicariously and offering contradictory advice. 'You must *give*, for God's sake, *give*!' 'Keep them guessing, Ruthie! Always keep the buggers guessing!' When I tried to evade her questions by pretending I was tired she would say, 'You've no business to be tired at your age. What's the matter with you? I never know whether you've enjoyed yourself or not: I hope *they* know.'

I always had enjoyed the parties, hadn't I? I didn't come home like other girls, tearful because I had been overlooked; or rapturously excited and subsequently

116

terribly let down. I was the one who always got the mixture right. And if I was a little anxious when I returned to the house, was there anything so unusual about that?

The telephone rang and I was glad of its intervention. It was Iris to know whether I was all right. I said I seemed to be having 'a reaction' and that I wouldn't be in for the rest of the week. She said that it was natural that I should have a reaction and to stay away and take things easily; I must not think about the office. Then she asked about several of the case files and whether I had got the appointment letters out for the following week. She was on the telephone for a long time. When I went back to bed Punter came up to tell me how desperate he was for the Hamiltons' bitch and to plead with me to let him out. In the afternoon, Mrs. James, our daily woman, came to clean the house. She made me a cup of tea and hovered in the doorway, recounting the latest village gossip. I could tell that I would have to postpone being really ill for another day. I got up, washed, dressed, and took Punter for a walk in the opposite direction to the Hamiltons' house.

It was a warm day with rather a lot of cloud and I felt tired and heavy. I had to keep Punter on the lead until we got down to the river. When I got back to the house I was exhausted. I sat in the sitting-room and went to sleep.

The next two days passed in much the same manner. Eleanor came to stay at the week-end. My father had told her that I was not well. She said that she would 'take over for a few days'. She said this deliberately and observed my reaction carefully. Our ability to get on together was a factor which had to be taken into account when considering how far to commit herself in her relationship with my father.

The building of relationships is hard, however, and I was not prepared to help with this one. Eleanor wanted

117

to see to what extent we could co-operate; but I left everything to her: she had, after all, said that she would 'take over'. I sat in a deck-chair in the garden. My father brought my meals to me on a tray, watched thoughtfully by Eleanor from the kitchen window. At tea-time, he said to me, 'Eleanor is quite surprising, isn't she?'

'In what way?'

'She's much more domesticated than I imagined.'

'I don't find that surprising,' I said indifferently. 'She's always had a place of her own to run.'

He looked uneasy. I closed my eyes and let my head roll to one side. He was planning to marry Eleanor. I would be needed to cement the marriage, to prove to him by my acceptance that it was all right. Well, I wasn't going to do it.

In the evening, I took Punter down to the river and walked along the tow-path. There were quite a lot of people there, boys fishing, families packing up picnic baskets, couples on their way to The Anglers' Rest. Someone called my name. I turned round and saw Iris walking towards me accompanied by her son. 'You remember Julian?' she said. He was tall and thin and gave an impression of lowering energy. He looked as though his mother was a continual source of exasperation to him.

'We're going to The Angler,' Iris said. 'Do come with us.'

I hesitated, thinking that my father might worry if I did not come back soon. But I told myself that that was a problem with which Eleanor could cope, and I agreed to have a drink with them.

The tow-path was narrow, so Julian and Iris walked in front. Iris kept a pace ahead of Julian and whenever he lengthened his stride she quickened her pace. Suddenly, he stopped short and I nearly bumped into him. Iris turned, surprised.

'You're doing it again,' he said plaintively. 'Why can't you walk level with anyone?'

'I'll walk with Ruth if you are going to be so silly.'

She walked beside me, but keeping a pace ahead. It seemed that, for her, the element of competition could never be absent. It was impossible not to react and I found myself walking more slowly.

'Andrew and Julian have been arguing so much that I came out with Julian to separate them,' she said. 'Julian is a revolutionary; his family's bourgeois, middle-class life style sickens him, doesn't it, Julian? But Andrew is just finishing at university so he's busy coming to terms with the capitalist society. He says he won't look at a job that starts below eight thousand. It was eight thousand, wasn't it, Julian?'

Julian muttered something that sounded obscene.

'I keep pointing out to Andrew that if he wants that kind of money he should have gone into computers. With an arts degree he'll be lucky to get a job.'

I stopped and threw a stone in the river for Punter. 'What about teaching?' I asked.

'It will probably come to that, but I don't like to be too discouraging at this stage.'

'You really are disgusting,' Julian said loudly.

The tow-path was widening now and we could walk three abreast; Iris and Julian competed for the lead with me and Punter trailing. Iris said, 'Disgusting perhaps, but a fact. People go into teaching if they can't get anything more rewarding. I know all about that.'

'We're not going to have all that about your father putting you into the teacher training factory, are we?'

'I had four brothers and they all went to university . . .'

'And all your sons are going to university and you were just a teacher and had to study psychology by candlelight! Oh Mum, don't get on to that now!'

By this time we had reached the garden at The Anglers' Rest. All the tables were occupied, so Iris and I

sat on the river bank while Julian stalked off to fetch
drinks. Iris watched him with an odd, baffled expression.
Was she thinking of the cost to her of child-bearing? I
thought of my mother and the farmer.

'It's a good job we met you,' Iris said. 'We are getting
across each other. I shall be glad when he's at university.
But he's not sixteen yet.'

'Should he be getting our drinks?'

'He looks older. They all do nowadays, don't they?' She
looked enviously at the young people lying on the grass. I
could not decide whether she was more vulnerable out of
the office or whether I was projecting my own feelings on
to her.

The river bank was steep here which was a pity because
I would like to have taken off my shoes and dangled my
feet in the water. Instead, I looked down into the water
while Iris talked.

'It's true that I wanted to be a missionary. I think the
idea probably came to me when I was up the apple tree.'
Julian returned with drinks and she said, 'I have been trying to explain it to Julian, but he gets cross.' Although
she made these remarks about Julian, she was by her
manner excluding him from the conversation rather than
drawing him into it.

'I don't know why you keep on about that apple tree.'
He spoke loudly and angrily, not, it seemed to me, because he was ill-natured but because he had devised no
other way of attracting her attention.

'That was when I decided I wanted to be a missionary,'
Iris said to me. 'Only there wasn't God.'

'*Of course* there wasn't God.'

'Yes, I know this annoys you, Julian; but that is because you don't try to follow what I am saying. You
should be prepared to talk about religion without losing
your temper.' In spite of the anger and resentment between them, I knew that they loved each other because I

120

felt their pain. 'It *is* a limiting factor, there being no God. I had a God's eye view of things up in that apple tree. There they were, my father and brothers, foreshortened and ineffective; I felt I could hold them in my hand; move them this way or that, change their lives. I felt very tender and responsible.'

'You're making it all up,' Julian said. 'You pelted them with apples.'

'It was after that, when I was in bed, that this yearning to change people came over me. I thought how tremendously exciting it would be to bring salvation to a subject race. But there is no satisfactory substitute for God when it comes to salvation. If you are bringing health and education you have to work in well-supervised units and if it's political salvation you've got to belong to a party; it is only the religious who can peddle salvation with a minimum of interference and no fear of being held accountable.'

Julian, who was sitting cross-legged with his beer on the ground in front of him, sniggered in embarrassment and said, 'Why couldn't you have been an explorer if you wanted to go it alone so much?'

'There were no undiscovered territories.'

'But there might have been some subject races that you could have dominated. That's what you want, Mum, domination! You're power mad.'

'When you come to think about it,' Iris turned to me with an air of confidentiality, 'all the great escape routes have been blocked for us. There are no colonies and . . .'

'All talk!' Julian interjected fiercely. 'Talk, talk, talk, you don't mean any of it . . .'

'. . . and the developing nations don't want us. We are thrown back on drugs and . . .'

'Thrown back on yourself!' he hooted triumphantly. 'Yourself, yourself, always yourself.'

'My round.' It seemed to me that this dangerous

121

shadow play in which they were indulging could not be resolved without injury. 'Drink up!' I made a movement to rise and Punter came across to me.

'On the contrary,' Iris turned on Julian, 'All my life I have had to put other people and their needs first.'

'You enjoy getting a hold on other people's needs; but you won't share yours with them. That's why you wouldn't come to stay in that commune with me.'

'We're not going to start that again, Julian. The people in that commune hadn't worked out their aims or . . .'

'They were doing the same sort of thing that you do in your clinic, only it was much more spontaneous and . . .'

'There's rather more to the healing process than eating health foods and weaving your own clothes with a spell of transcendental meditation thrown in for good measure.'

'You don't give a fuck about healing! It's just a game of forfeits, what goes on in your clinic.'

'I don't know about forfeits, but . . .'

'When you played forfeits as a child the person who was caught out had to tell a secret, didn't you tell me that, didn't you? And that's what happens at your clinic; you hand over advice in return for secrets.'

'However long have you been storing that up, I wonder? You really are becoming very manipulative.'

'Manipulative? Me!' Julian began to get to his feet and in doing so made a movement towards me. Punter, who had become increasingly agitated as the argument intensified, misjudged his intentions and leapt at him. He was not a fierce dog, but he was heavy. Julian overbalanced and fell headlong in the river. Punter went in after him, whether to effect a rescue or to complete the assault was not clear.

'Call him off!' Iris said to me.

'He won't bite,' I said. 'Retrieving dogs never do.'

'Julian doesn't need retrieving. He can swim.'

Nevertheless, she hitched up her skirt and edged down

the bank. I felt I should do the same, although I could see that Punter and Julian were heading towards the bank on separate courses. Iris lost her balance; she slewed to one side and lurched against a fisherman whose line had already been fouled by Julian. 'I'm so sorry!' She righted herself, knocking his food hamper into the water in the process.

One or two other fishermen who had been having a dull evening up to now abandoned their lines and waded out to give Julian assistance which he did not need. He was humiliated, furious with his mother, and incapable of behaving graciously. As soon as he reached firm ground, he shook off his rescuers and strode down the tow-path. Iris was engaged in conversation with the fisherman who was trying to salvage his hamper.

'I'm terribly sorry, but you could see it was an accident . . .'

'Why didn't you go in the bar if you wanted to shout and yammer all the evening?'

Punter clambered up the bank and shook himself briskly.

Iris said, 'Let me buy you a drink.' She turned to Julian's rescuers who seemed more willing to take up her offer. 'What will you have?'

I waited a few minutes to give Julian a good start before putting on Punter's lead and setting off for home.

It had all been much less dangerous than I had imagined. In spite of their aggressiveness there was some element in their relationship which kept them safe. I had had about as much understanding of the situation as Punter. I still did not understand. In particular, I did not understand Julian. It was not just that I would never have talked to my parents like that; I would never have thought about them in that way.

When I got back to the house my father said, 'You've had a long walk.'

'Punter wanted a swim.'

He hesitated, not satisfied with the answer; his eyes searched my face, seeking permission to be concerned and loving but afraid of a rebuff. I decided that I must be more like Julian; Julian, if abrasive, was positive in his attitude. I said to my father, 'You are a silly old thing. I've only been out about an hour.' My voice sounded loud and up hockey sticks. He looked startled, not unreasonably. I abandoned the positive approach and said persuasively, 'You mustn't worry about me.'

'But I do worry about you.'

'You never used to.'

'But you're all I've got now.' He was quite testy. 'So naturally I worry.'

'Oh darling, I'm sorry.' I flung my arms round him. 'I love you. I know I'm beastly sometimes, but I do love you.' I hoped that he would say he loved me, too, and we might both have a little cry, but he patted my head and said, 'You'd better not go back to work next week.' He was no longer in a demonstrative mood: co-ordination seemed to be our problem as much as anything.

'Better tell Eleanor you're here. I think supper is spoiling.' He frowned, mock severe, making a scapegoat of Eleanor.

I went into the kitchen where Eleanor was adjusting the position of dishes in the oven. Her face was a dark wine-red, perhaps from the heat of the oven.

'Are you going back to work on Monday?' She sounded very much my aunt and I remembered how little I had liked her when I was a child. I shrugged my shoulders.

'You'll have to get a doctor's certificate if you stay away any longer, won't you?'

'I don't suppose he'll refuse me one,' I answered, resenting her tone. 'I'm not often away from work.'

She took plates down from the rack. 'Do you feel you can eat?'

124

'I expect so; I'm not sick, just tired.'

'I'm sorry if I sound unsympathetic, but sometimes we're better off at work even if we don't feel a hundred per cent.'

She's afraid 'we' are going to have a breakdown, I thought. I said, 'I'll see what the doctor has to say.'

'Suppose he gives you a week off, would you go away? It would probably do you good to get out of this house.'

'I'm tired. I don't want to make plans.'

She said sharply, 'You'll have to make plans sometime in your life, Ruth.'

'Oh sod off, Eleanor!'

She was startled and so was I. She occupied herself with removing dishes from the oven and I tried to make amends by carrying plates into the dining-room.

My late arrival had unsettled my father and he had been further disturbed by a television programme on the third world. Until recently he had been liberal in his attitudes and he had kept up to date in his knowledge of current affairs, politics, art and music. For a good many men, the learning process seems to stop with school or university; many of my friends' fathers had put ideas away along with their student gear. I had been proud of my father. My boy friends had enjoyed talking to him, he listened to them with interest and put his own views diffidently. There was nothing diffident about him now. He was angry and bewildered and he made bitter, destructive comments about the government's policy on Northern Ireland and Rhodesia; he condemned the new purchases by the Tate; he deplored the National Theatre's choice of play and the B.B.C.'s late night music programmes. Anything which demanded a change in his way of looking at life seemed not only to anger, but to frighten him. He was letting go his hold on modern life. He had often criticised Eleanor because she was a dissatisfied person; but tonight he looked to her for support. He found her company congenial because they could grumble together and he seemed to look forward to a union of discontent.

Eleanor, to my surprise, was not prepared to accommodate him. After a few non-committal replies, she said, 'They're not all as bad as that, surely? I don't think you would describe Stoppard as decadent, would you?'

'I wouldn't describe him as a playwright.' My father looked at her severely. 'I don't go to the theatre to listen to long monologues about Lenin, do you?'

Eleanor looked over his left shoulder, musing. 'I remember being rather moved by that.'

'Moved?' He put his knife and fork down and stared at her in pained incredulity. 'Moved by someone sitting in a corner of the stage recounting reminiscences you could go and read for yourself in the public library if you had a few hours to waste!'

'And I thought the ending was extremely moving.'

'The ending!'

'Extremely.' Eleanor took a sip of wine and savoured it appreciatively.

'I wouldn't have said it *did* end. It just came to a halt.'

We finished our fish, which was haddock in a tasty garlic sauce, in silence. My father several times glanced sideways at Eleanor as though reappraising her. She had been tractable in the garden and perhaps he had expected that she would accept his lead in other matters. When she had served a lemon soufflé, he said, 'You'll tell me you liked the Tate's bricks, next.'

'No, they were beyond me. But that was a long time ago . . .'

'It wasn't such a very long time.' He was offended by the idea that his measure of time was different to hers. 'And as for saying that they were beyond you, you surely can't be serious? You're much too sensible to accept the